'I'd just like to
changed.'

Rebecca's mouth fell open.

'I know you recognise me. It's been quite a while, hasn't it, Rebecca? Did you think I didn't remember you?' His voice was as soft and smooth as melted chocolate. It made her dizzy, a response which she immediately put down to confusion.

Nicholas gave Rebecca a slow smile that made her pulse race. 'You haven't the sort of face that's easily forgotten. But I don't expect you to back out of our arrangement because of our past little liaison.'

His dark eyes held hers unwaveringly and she finally realised what she'd let herself in for...

Cathy Williams is Trinidadian and was brought up on the twin islands of Trinidad and Tobago. She was awarded a scholarship to study in Britain, and came to Exeter University in 1975 to continue her studies into the great loves of her life: languages and literature. It was there that Cathy met her husband, Richard. Since they married Cathy has lived in England, originally in the Thames Valley but now in the Midlands. Cathy and Richard have three small daughters.

Recent titles by the same author:

WIFE FOR HIRE

BY
CATHY WILLIAMS

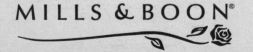

MILLS & BOON®

*First published in Great Britain 1999
Harlequin Mills & Boon Limited,
Eton House, 18-24 Paradise Road, Richmond, Surrey TW9 1SR*

© Cathy Williams 1999

ISBN 0 263 81929 9

*Set in Times Roman 10½ on 12 pt.
01-0002-48436 C1*

*Printed and bound in Spain
by Litografía Rosés, S.A., Barcelona*

CHAPTER ONE

FROM the very moment that Rebecca Ryan opened her eyes that morning, she knew that the next few hours were going to be the worst of her teaching career.

She was not, by nature, prone to dramatic flights of imagination, but for a few brief seconds she heartily wished that she could shut her eyes and make the day go away; then she climbed out of bed and headed for the bathroom. Normally, this was her most relaxing time of the day. That long, leisurely soak in the bath before she opened the door of her small but comfortable school quarters, and braced herself for the challenges confronting anyone courageous enough to teach in an all-girls boarding-school. Or, as Mrs Williams, the principal, once put it, to exercise skilful manipulation of the homesick, the pre-pubescent, the adolescent, the hormonal and the pre-menstrual, whilst trying to educate to the highest possible standard.

Rebecca loved every minute of it.

Except, she thought, settling into the bath water, for to-day. Today she wished that she had mulled over her career options a bit more thoroughly at the age of twenty-one, and decided in favour of something slightly less stress-inducing, such as copy typist.

She sighed deeply and allowed her mind to scuttle over the past thirty-six hours.

There should be a tablet you could take to get rid of unpleasant situations, she thought. There would be a huge market for it. Just swallow two special, new, improved paracetamol capsules and let your problems fade conveniently away.

In the absence of any such panacea, she mentally worked out how she would deal with the problem staring her in the face. Part of it had already been handled, and she had emerged shocked, bruised but, generally speaking, still in good working order.

Part two of the problem, which she estimated was probably a mere one hour's drive away from the school, would have to be dealt with as pragmatically as possible. Parents, she knew from experience, were not particularly reasonable when it came to dealing with their children's misdemeanours. They were prone, initially, to disbelief, then to self-recrimination, and finally, in a few instances, to complete denial of all blame by placing it squarely on whomever happened to be handy, usually the teacher.

Rebecca, whose height waged a constant battle with the dimensions of most baths, stuck her feet out at the bottom, wriggled her toes and decided that, if Mrs Williams refused to allow her the luxury of sitting through the uncomfortable interview in relative silence, she would be firm, practical, sympathetic and as implacable as a rock.

She would be very careful not to let her wayward tongue get the better of her. She would keep all personal opinion to herself. She would smile a lot, with more than a hint of compassion, and she would not presume to preach to someone she didn't know from Adam on his methods of fathering. She would close her mind to every word Emily Parr had uttered to her on the subject of her father, because teenagers could be quite unreliable when it came to descriptions of their home lives, and she would do as little as possible to upset any apple carts.

That resolved, she contemplated what she should wear for the meeting. Normally, as a teacher, she invariably opted for the most comfortable clothing she could find. Loose skirts and tops, flat shoes, muted colours. From as far back as she could remember, she had always tried to wear things that diminished her size. Five feet ten inches was tall enough, but add to that a generous bustline and curves that never seemed appropriate for the role of teacher, and what remained was something, she considered, fairly Amazonian.

Today, she decided, she would take advantage of her height to ward off any attacks Emily's father might have in store for her. She knew that she frequently intimidated men. There was nothing about her at all that begged for their protective instincts. If anything, with some of the men she had dated in the past, *she* had ended up feeling protective. She had long ago assumed that the only men she attracted were the ones who were turned on by a dominant female. Or at least by a woman they considered would fit the role of the dominant female. It was useless telling them that the last thing she wanted was to take command or, God forbid, mother them.

She slipped on a dark grey suit, which was as prepossessing on her as a cold sore but succeeded in making her look rather intimidating, and stuck on a pair of two-inch high-heel court shoes which she had to dust down from lack of use. Then she stood in front of the mirror and surveyed the net result with a critical eye.

Definitely the outfit for a potentially difficult situation, she decided. And, from what she had heard about Emily's father from Mrs Williams, she would need all the superficial help she could get her hands on.

He was, she had worked out, not one of life's easygoing characters. For a start, he had made only one appearance in the two years his daughter had been at the school, and that had been to complain about her grades. Mrs Williams, recalling the incident, had blanched at the memory of it, and it took a great deal for Mrs Williams to lose her legendary calm.

So how he was going to react to this major body blow he would be dealt in a little under an hour was enough to make anyone shudder with apprehension.

Rebecca gazed thoughtfully at her reflection and was, for once, grateful for what confronted her. A woman of imposing height and stature, face attractive but well played down so that the firm jawline and widely spaced blue eyes looked strongly determined, and with her shoulder-length auburn hair tortured into something she hoped resembled a bun at the back, she looked every inch the sort of person that other people should consider very carefully before antagonising.

And her curves were well concealed under the boxy grey jacket. Curves and grim-lipped severity did not make the best of companions.

Fifteen minutes later she was striding confidently towards the principal's office, glancing in at the classes in progress and mentally hoping that her own class was being well behaved for Mr Emscote, the English teacher, who had a tendency to wilt when confronted with too many high-spirited teenage girls.

Mrs Williams was waiting for her in the office, standing by the window, and looking fairly agitated.

'He should be here in a short while. Please sit, Rebecca.' She sighed wearily and took her place in the chair behind the large mahogany desk. 'I've told Sylvia to make sure that we're not interrupted. Has Emily been to see you again?'

'No.' Rebecca shook her head. 'I think she decided that I needed a bit of a breather after the shock. How did she react to your talk with her?'

Another weary sigh, this time more pronounced. 'She didn't. React, that is. Barely said a word and looked utterly pleased with herself in that insufferably insolent manner she has.'

Rebecca knew precisely the insufferably insolent manner to which Mrs Williams was referring. It involved a bored expression, stifled yawns and eyes that drifted around the room as though searching for something slightly more exciting to materialise from the woodwork. She was the perfect rebel and, because of it, had a league of adoring supporters who, thankfully, while admiring her antics, were not quite foolhardy enough to imitate them.

'Did you mention anything to her father about…why he was asked to come here?'

'I thought it best to do that on a face-to-face basis.'

Shame, Rebecca thought. He might have simmered down if he had had a day to mull over the facts.

'I've gathered all the relevant school reports on Emily, so that he can read through them, and I've also collated the numerous incident reports as well. Quite a number, considering that the child hasn't been with us very long.' She sat back in the chair, a small, thin bespectacled woman in her forties with the tenacity and perseverance of a bull-dog, and shook her head. 'Such a shame. Such a clever child. It certainly makes one wonder what the point of brilliance is when motivation doesn't play a part. With a different attitude, she could have achieved a great deal.'

'She's had a…challenging home life, Mrs Williams. I personally feel, as I said to you before, that Emily's rebelliousness is all an act. A ploy to hide her own insecurities.'

'Yes, well, I suggest you keep your opinions to yourself, Rebecca,' the principal said in a warning voice. 'There's no point in muddying the waters with a post-mortem on why this whole unfortunate business happened in the first place. Aside from which, she's not the first girl to have endured her parents' divorce and all the fallout from it. And other girls do not react by…' she looked down at one of the sheets of paper '…smoking through the window of a dorm, falsifying sick notes to the infirmary so that she can go into town, climbing up a tree and remaining there for a day just to watch us all run around like headless chickens looking for her… The list goes on…'

'Yes, I know, but…' Rebecca could feel herself getting hot under the collar of her crisply starched white blouse, which she had unearthed from the furthermost reaches of her wardrobe and now felt so uncomfortable that she was seriously regretting having put it on in the first place.

'No buts, Rebecca. This is an immovable situation and it will do no good to try and analyse it into making sense. The facts are as they stand and Emily's father will have to accept them whether he cares to or not.'

'And Emily?' Rebecca asked with concern. 'What happens to her now?'

'That will be something that must be sorted out between herself and her father.'

'She doesn't *have* a relationship with her father.'

'I would advise you to be a bit sceptical about what she says on that front,' Mrs Williams told her sharply. 'We both know that Emily can be very creative with the truth.'

'But the facts speak for themselves…' Rebecca found herself leaning forward, about to disobey her first rule of command, which was to be as immovable as a rock and launch into a fiery defence of her pupil, when there was a knock on the door, and Sylvia poked her head round.

'Mr Knight is here, Mrs Williams,' she said with her usual gusto.

Mr Knight? Rebecca frowned. Why was his surname

different from that of his daughter? References to him had always been as Emily's father, and it hadn't occurred to her that he might not be Mr Parr.

'That's fine, Sylvia. Would you show him in, please? And no interruptions, *please*. I shall deal with anything that crops up *after* Mr Knight has left.'

'Of course.' Sylvia's expression changed theatrically from beaming good humour to grave understanding, but as soon as she had vacated the doorway they could both hear her trill to Emily's father that he could go in now, and could he please inform her how he would like his coffee.

Rebecca wondered whether he would be disconcerted by the personal assistant's eccentric mannerisms—most people who didn't know her were—but his deep voice, wafting through the door, was controlled and chillingly assured.

Stupidly, because her role in the room was simply to impart information, she felt her stomach muscles clench as he walked through the door, then a wave of colour flooded her cheeks.

Mrs Williams had risen to her feet and was perfunctorily shaking his hand, and it was only when they both turned to her that Rebecca sprang up and held out her hand in polite greeting.

Emily's father was strikingly tall, strikingly forbidding and strikingly good-looking. Even wearing heels, she was forced to look up at him. She didn't know what she had expected of him. Someone older, for a start, and with the military bearing of the typical household dictator who had no time for family but a great deal for work.

This man was raven-haired, dark-eyed and the angular features of his face all seemed to blend together to give an impression of power, self-assurance and cool disregard for the rest of the human race.

And the worst of it was that she recognised him. Seventeen years on, she recognised him. At sixteen she had been as knocked sideways by the man he had been then as she was now by the man he had become.

Knight. Not the most run-of-the-mill name in the world, but even in those fleeting seconds when the principal had referred to him by name it had not occurred to her that the man she was about to meet was the same Nicholas Knight whom she had briefly known.

She could feel her hand tremble as he gripped it in his, then she pulled away quickly and sat back down, watching to see whether there were any signs of recognition on his face.

None. Of course. As she might have expected. She lowered her eyes and heard him ask, as he sat down facing them both, if they could kindly explain what was of sufficient urgency to bring him here.

'I was due to leave for New York this morning,' he said, crossing his legs. 'This is all highly inconvenient. I don't know what Emily's done this time, but I'm sure it could have been dealt with in the usual way.'

He had a deep, lazy voice and watchful manner which seemed to convey the message that, however much you knew, he knew infinitely more. Rebecca suspected that her dress code would not be having the desired effect. Seventeen years ago, he would have been amused at the thought of female intimidation. Now, from what she could see, it would barely register.

She sneaked a glance at him from under her lashes and felt the same illicit thrill she had felt when she had first set eyes on him at the local charity function all those years ago. Even then he had had the sort of commanding presence that made heads swing around for a second look.

'I'm afraid not, Mr Knight.' The principal removed her spectacles and leant forward, resting both elbows on the desk. 'Emily has quite surpassed herself this time, which is why we felt it wise to summon you immediately.'

'Even though we realise what a very busy man you are,' Rebecca said sweetly—a remark which was greeted by the merest thinning of his lips. She felt his dark eyes course over her and calmly refused to look away.

It was beginning to sting a little that he obviously did not remember her. True, their acquaintance had been short-lived—barely a fortnight from beginning to end—but she wasn't *that* forgettable, was she?

Of course, she knew, deep down, why he didn't recall her. Unimportant blips were hardly the foundations of solid, long-lasting memories, and her presence in his life had been an unimportant blip, even though he had remained in her head for many months afterwards. To him, she had been little more than the girl from the wrong side of the tracks with whom he had planned on having a bit of harmless fun before she pre-empted him by walking away.

'What's the problem *this time*?' he asked in a world-weary voice. 'What has she broken?' He reached inside his jacket pocket to extract his cheque-book, and Rebecca gave an automatic grimace of distaste, which he caught and held.

'Do you have a problem?' he enquired politely, looking at her. 'I take it from the affronted expression on your face that you disapprove of something?'

Rebecca decided that she would abandon her vow of silence on the grounds that keeping too much in was fine in theory, but in practice would probably give her irreversible high blood pressure.

'Not everything can be sorted out with a cheque-book, Mr Knight.' People like him thought otherwise. She was fully aware of that. He had spent his entire life cushioned by wealth and he would automatically assume that there was nothing that could not be rectified if enough cash was flung at it.

So his daughter misbehaved, or wrecked a few things, or stepped out of line—well, let's just sort it out by adding a new wing to the school library, shall we?

He very slowly closed the cheque-book and slipped it back into his jacket pocket, not taking his eyes off her face.

'Ah. I see where we're heading. Before my daughter's slip-up, whatever that might be, is to be discussed, I'm first to be subjected to a ham-fisted analysis of why she did what she did. Time is money, Miss Ryan, so if you're bursting to get your prepared speech out, then I suggest you make it fast so that I can sort this business out and be on my way.'

'We're not in the business of lecturing to our parents, Mr Knight,' Mrs Williams said firmly, before Rebecca could be tempted into taking him at his word and delivering a thorough, no-stone-unturned lecture on precisely what she thought of him.

'In which case, you might pass the message on to your assistant. She looks as though she's about to explode at any moment now.'

'Miss Ryan,' she said, throwing her a gimlet-eyed look, 'is an experienced and immensely good teacher. There is *absolutely no way* that she would allow herself to voice her private opinions.'

Rebecca nearly grinned at that. They both knew that

voicing opinions was something she was remarkably good at.

'I wouldn't dream of it,' she agreed demurely, and he raised his eyebrows sceptically at her tone of voice.

That particular tendency was still there, she noticed. The first time she had seen him, he had been lounging at the makeshift bar in the village hall. The dance floor had been packed to the seams with youngsters, and she had been standing to one side with a drink in her hand, miserably watching everyone have fun and thinking that she should have dispensed with her frock and her high heels which made her feel stuffy and over-large, rather like a sofa deposited at random in a china shop. All her friends were so petite, so feminine and so utterly unlike her.

Then she had caught his eye and he had raised his eyebrows very much as he had done just then, as though he could cut straight through to what she had been thinking, as though they had momentarily shared some private joke together.

'Good.' He reverted his attention to Mrs Williams now. 'Now that I am to be spared an unnecessary lecture, perhaps we could stop beating around the bush and you could just tell me why I've been summoned here at such short notice. What has my daughter done this time?'

'Perhaps you could explain, Miss Ryan?'

Thanks very much, Rebecca thought wryly to herself.

'Two nights ago Emily came to see me, Mr Knight.'

'She *came to see you*?' He frowned, perplexed. 'She left the building at night to pay you a visit? Is this normal procedure? For a child of sixteen to be allowed out on her own into the town so that she can *visit* a teacher? Aren't there certain rules and regulations in operation around here?'

Call me a fool, Rebecca thought to herself, but I smell

a very difficult situation ahead. She wished she were a million miles away, lying on a beach somewhere, recovering from the stress of the copy-typing job she should have gone for.

'If you could let me finish, Mr Knight, *without butting in*?' She made sure not to look at the principal when she said this, but even with her eyes strenuously averted she could easily imagine the look of warning that would have crossed Mrs Williams's face.

'I happen to *live* on the premises.'

'We have what are called house mothers here,' the principal explained. 'Each dormitory section is manned by one. They basically live here and supervise the children out of school hours, make sure that everything is running smoothly. It's not uncommon for them to have visits during the night, especially by the younger ones who are new and perhaps a little homesick.'

'You're a young woman. Why on earth would you choose to live in a boarding-school?'

'As I was saying, Mr Knight,' Rebecca carried on, overriding his question with the single-minded intent of a bulldozer, 'Emily came to see me to talk about a rather...unfortunate situation.' She glanced at Mrs Williams for support and the other woman nodded encouragingly.

Emily's father, on the other hand, looked slightly less encouraging. His face was grim, unreadable and frankly terrifyingly forbidding.

'I'm waiting,' he said at last, when an uncomfortable silence had begun to thicken around them as Rebecca searched for the most tactful way of saying what she had to say. 'Is she on drugs?'

'No.' She inhaled deeply, adopted her sternest expression and clasped her hands on her knees. 'I'm sure you've been made aware, Mr Knight, over the past couple of years, that your daughter has been…'

'Bloody difficult. Why don't you just come right out with what you have to say, Miss Ryan? The facts don't go away, however much you try and sugar-coat them. Yes. I have been all too aware of what she has managed to get up to. It hasn't made pretty reading and I needn't tell you that I've been losing patience fast.'

Charming attitude to adopt, Rebecca thought, directing a meaningless smile at him and suppressing the urge to clout him over the head.

'To be honest, I was a little stunned when she knocked on my door at two in the morning. Emily isn't one for confiding in her teachers. She enjoys being a law unto herself, doesn't like anyone to glimpse her vulnerabilities, and before you object to what I'm saying I can assure you that *all* girls of sixteen are vulnerable, whatever air of bravado they might choose to wear.'

'I'll take you at your word, Miss Ryan. I have no experience of teenage girls.'

'Including your own,' Rebecca countered before she could censor her thoughts, and he shot her a hard, cold look.

'Just carry on with the facts, Miss Ryan, and keep your thoughts to yourself.'

'I think that what Miss Ryan is trying to say,' Miss Williams took up hastily, 'is that we are quite accustomed to dealing with unruly girls and we tend towards leniency in most cases. A stern talking-to usually does the trick. Boarding-school can seem restricting to some of our girls, at least initially. They are disoriented, and they react, occasionally, without thinking. These problems are by no means frequent, but they do occur, and we all recognise how to deal with them.'

'Fine.' He had not glanced in the direction of the principal. His eyes had remained focused on Rebecca the whole time. She began to feel hot and uneasy. She could also feel her ridiculous bun beginning to slip out of place, and she wondered whether she could halt its progress downwards by keeping her head very, very still.

She decided, as he continued to stare at her with the off-putting concentration of someone trying to move an immovable object by exerting will-power, that time had honed that natural self-assurance that had first attracted her into obnoxious arrogance. There was no other word for it. The man was a pig.

Was he *totally* incapable of taking *any* responsibility for his daughter's behaviour? Did he imagine that young girls of sixteen operated in emotional vacuums?

'She was in quite a state,' Rebecca confessed. 'I made her sit down, and she told me... I'm afraid to tell you, Mr Knight, that your daughter informs us that...that she's pregnant.'

The word fell into the silence like a stone. Seconds passed. Minutes. He said nothing.

'Perhaps you can understand now why we felt we had to get you up here, Mr Knight,' the principal said gently. 'I realise that this must come as a shock to you...'

'How the hell was this allowed to happen?' His words were soft and sharp, but they still managed to reverberate around the room like a thunderclap. He turned to look at Rebecca. 'You say that you live on the premises so that you can make sure that everything is running smoothly. Well, you haven't managed to do a very good job, have you? What were you doing while my teenage daughter was slinking along the corridors at night and heading into town to meet some man? And do we know the identity of this bastard?'

Under the controlled voice, she could sense a man who wanted to kill and, however much she disliked what she had seen of him so far, she could sympathise with him. He must feel as though a bomb had been dropped on him from a very great height.

'First of all Emily isn't on my floor…'

'Then why would she come to you with her problems?'

'Because…'

'Perhaps,' Mrs Williams said in a conciliatory tone of voice, 'because Miss Ryan is one of our younger members of staff. Many of the girls turn to her for advice. She's popular…'

'Yes, well, a glowing appraisal of Miss Ryan's character isn't what I'm after right now. What I want—' he leaned forward, resting his elbows on his knees, and the slight shift in position made Rebecca instinctively cringe back into the chair, causing further damage to her already precarious hairdo '—is a bloody explanation!'

'Emily hasn't gone into details, Mr Knight,' Rebecca answered. Her hands were shaking and she steadied them on her lap, linking her fingers together. 'She won't say who the boy in question is and she won't tell us how it happened. It's highly unlikely that she slipped out at night. The doors would have been very securely locked to prevent the girls from doing just that sort of thing and there is a night watchman on the premises. It's far more likely that she met him during the day, probably on a weekend when the girls are allowed a certain amount of freedom once they get to a certain age. They are not kept padlocked here. We hope that they have the right moral codes instilled that will guide—'

'Oh, why don't we just cut through all this claptrap? What you're telling me here is that you accept no responsibility for what's happened! It's unfortunate that a child's life has been ruined, but as far as you're concerned you intend to wash your hands of it and put it all down to experience. Am I right?'

Why on earth doesn't he direct this tirade at the principal? Rebecca thought distractedly. Why does he keep staring at me as though I've single-handedly engineered all of this? She squirmed uncomfortably, aware that he had struck close to a chord. Of course, it was an awful thing to have happened, but at the end of the day Emily would be expelled and, in time, forgotten.

'Of course that's not what we're saying!' she snapped angrily. 'It's distressing, not least for your daughter! But it's happened, and she's going to have to live with the consequences! Berating us, and berating her, isn't going to make the situation change, Mr Knight. It's just going to make it all the harder for her to cope with it!'

'So what happens now?' he threw at her. He glanced from her to the principal, his eyes cold with rage. 'Would either of you ladies care to tell me? No, allow me to have a stab at guessing. She's to pack her bags and leave the premises immediately. Her education will seize up and, wherever she ends up, may it all be a salutary lesson for one and all! Am I on target here?'

'What choice do we have, Mr Knight?' Mrs Williams said wearily. She looked exhausted, Rebecca thought. It had not been a wonderful thirty-six hours for her. This was the sort of incident that could wreak havoc amongst the school. Parents would be alarmed. The fallout was not worth thinking about, and it would be no use to suggest to concerned mothers and fathers that Emily had been in a category of her own. A time bomb waiting to explode.

'We have no option *but* to ask you to remove Emily from the school. Naturally she will be given until the weekend to get her things in order.'

'Naturally…' His mouth twisted harshly, then he sighed and rubbed his eyes. 'So have neither of you *any* ideas on how this problem might be dealt with?' He shot an accusing eye in the principal's direction. 'Even if you sit stiff-backed in your chair and accept *no* responsibility for what's happened, this can't be the first time…'

'Absolutely the first time, Mr Knight. There are no precedents we can follow here.'

'She'll need your support,' Rebecca interjected, and he turned to her with a cynical glint.

'I must say that's going to be a trifle difficult to muster up. It's been impossible enough dealing with her since she came to me two years ago, but this is positively the last damned straw!'

That, Rebecca thought, was not quite the story that Emily had told her. In between her tears, she had bitterly informed her that her father had had zero time for her ever since she had been landed on him thanks to her mother's death in a skiing accident. She had had little contact with him as it was as a child. With her parents divorced when she was two, her mother had not encouraged father/daughter bonding. In fact, she had expressly forbidden it and had moved to the opposite side of the world in an attempt to avoid any such thing. He hadn't pursued her then, and ever since she had been returned to him he had chosen to ignore her because she was no more than a stranger who did not fit in with his lifestyle.

'So what do you intend to do?' Rebecca asked coolly. 'I don't believe homes for fallen women still exist.'

'That's a particularly constructive remark, isn't it, Miss Ryan?' he told her acidly. 'Any more where that came from?'

Rebecca blushed, furious with herself for voicing thoughts that were better kept to herself, and ashamed that in the midst of this painful and difficult situation she could find herself distracted by Nicholas Knight. He was some-one who was buried so deeply in her past that it surprised her to discover just how easily she could recover the image and the wounded feelings inflicted on her over a decade ago.

'I'm sorry,' she said sincerely. 'There was absolutely no call for that, and you're right, it wasn't constructive. What you might find constructive is if I tell you Emily is not the first teenager to find herself in this situation, and she can come out of it. She might leave this school, but there's no reason why her education has to come to an abrupt end because of it. She can be tutored at home. She's an in-credibly clever child and—who knows?—this might just be the thing that helps her find her way.'

'How pregnant…is she?' The distaste in his voice was audible and Rebecca shivered. Poor Emily, however down-right stupid she had been, was not going to find her father easily forgiving.

'Only just.'

'Meaning?'

'A week…overdue, apparently. But the pregnancy test, she informed me tearfully, was definitely positive. In fact, she said that she did two, just in case the first was wrong.'

'Home tutoring,' he said to himself. He stroked his chin with one finger, frowning, and Rebecca caught herself star-ing. She pulled herself up short and allowed her eyes to wander away from him. 'I suppose that's the only solution, isn't it?' he said to them. He looked at Mrs Williams for a while. 'Could you excuse us for a minute? There's some-thing I'd like to discuss in private with Miss Ryan.'

'Well…' The principal hesitated, taken aback by the request.

'I'm sure anything that needs to be discussed can be discussed in front of—'

'We'll be twenty minutes.' He gave them both a bland, impenetrable look and Rebecca watched in frustrated silence as Mrs Williams left the room, shutting the door behind her.

CHAPTER TWO

'HOME tutoring.' He sat back in his chair, crossed his legs and looked at her. 'Carry on.'

'Sorry?'

'You were giving a little pep talk on all the opportunities still available to a teenager who has been stupid enough to get herself pregnant. You mentioned home tutoring as an option.'

'Yes.' He had removed his jacket before entering the room, and now he slowly began to roll the sleeves of his shirt up, exposing strong forearms, black-haired, and lightly bronzed. Although he was English by birth, she remembered him telling her years ago that there was Greek blood in him. Lust had apparently got the better of common sense, and his maternal grandmother had shocked everyone by throwing caution, and her very British fiancé, to the winds and marrying the son of a Greek tycoon. The tale had amused him, had appealed to that element in him that rebelled against convention.

She dragged her eyes away from his wretched arms and fastened them on his face. 'Home tutoring. I didn't mention that because I felt any kind of obligation to point out a bright side to this whole sorry business. I mentioned it because it's a perfectly viable option, and actually I think Emily would do very well on it. She's incredibly bright. She picks things up very easily. It would more be a matter of steering her towards her exams, making sure that certain levels of work were maintained.

'I'm not saying that it would be a piece of cake for her,

or for her tutor for that matter. She'll still have to deal with all the ups and downs of the pregnancy, still have to come to terms with it, and she can be difficult.' Rebecca laughed a little. 'Possibly one of the bigger understatements of my lifetime. But she should be all right, at least academically, provided you find the right tutor. Someone patient, I think.'

'You didn't explain why my daughter chose you for her confidante.'

'Well...' Rebecca blushed '...as Mrs Williams said, I *am* one of the younger members of the staff here, and, well, I *do* pride myself on having a certain rapport with the girls. I do a fair amount of stuff with them after school hours. I run the amateur dramatic society, for example. Actually, that was about the only class that your daughter really seemed to enjoy. I think she liked being able to slip in and out of characters. Perhaps she found it relaxing.'

'Yes, that would make sense.' His mouth twisted cynically. 'Her mother was fond of amateur dramatics herself.' He laughed shortly. 'Probably runs in the genes.'

'Well, I wouldn't know about that,' Rebecca said vaguely.

'No. I don't suppose you would. You just know Emily as a child who joined your school approximately two years ago and has proved troublesome from day one. Do you ever take an interest in their backgrounds?'

He was looking at her curiously now, and there was something ever so slightly critical about his appraisal.

'To some extent,' she said stiffly. 'But if you imagine that I spend half my leisure time going through their personal records, reading up on what their parents do for a living, then no. I don't.'

'So you are unaware of the circumstances surrounding my daughter...'

'I know that her mother died two years ago…' Actually, she did have some idea of Emily's background from what the child had told her, but she had no intention of admitting that. Trust was something that teenagers held very dear, and she was not about to break Emily's.

'So you're not aware that she and I were divorced when Emily was only a toddler.'

'I don't see how this is relevant…to what we were discussing earlier, Mr Knight. Namely, home tutoring for your daughter.'

'Oh, but you were so quick to judge me earlier on, Miss Ryan,' he said smoothly, and a little caustically. 'I thought you would be eager to slot together the little mental puzzle you had formed of my relationship with Emily. I mean, there's no point in jumping to lots of amateur deductions if you only know the surface gloss, is there?'

'It's none of my business,' Rebecca said, blushing furiously. She pressed her head against the back of the chair in an attempt to stop her hair from unravelling totally. Why she had bothered with these ridiculously uncomfortable clothes, she had no idea. Nicholas Knight was about as intimidated by her as an elephant by a flea. And she felt as though she was suffocating in her jacket, which she had not had the foresight to remove from the beginning. 'Anyway, Mrs. Williams will be returning shortly…'

'But I'm sure she'll leave again if we're not quite finished.'

'Not quite finished with *what*? I don't think there's anything else I can tell you on the subject of home tutoring. If you like, I'm sure Mrs Williams can recommend a few people…' A few brave, intrepid people, she thought to herself. Emily would need brave and intrepid. She would need the sort of private tutor who did bungee jumping for fun in his spare time. Such creatures were thin on the ground.

'I shouldn't like to leave you with any deluded impressions of me, Miss Ryan. I know your conscience couldn't bear it if you thought that you were dispatching my daughter off to face a life of despair and misery at the hands of an unsympathetic, absentee father.'

'Why would I think that?'

'Because if Emily ran to you with tales of what had happened, then it's more than likely that she confided all about her unhappy family life.' He gave her a shrewd, knowing look. 'I wasn't born yesterday, you know.'

'Well, she just mentioned one or two things. In passing,' Rebecca answered feebly.

'Care to fill me in?'

'I *did* happen to know that you and your wife split up when she was two, and she was taken to Australia to live.'

'Did she also tell you that I did my damnedest to keep in touch, and that it was only years later that I was informed by her mother that every letter and present I had sent over the years had been shredded and destroyed? By which time she had been inculcated in the belief that I was the big bad wolf who had driven her innocent, victimised mother into a divorce she never wanted, and then, not content with that, had forced her to flee to the opposite ends of the earth?'

Not precisely, Rebecca thought. She couldn't quite understand why Nicholas Knight felt obliged to fill her in on any of this, but, as a teacher, she knew that she had a duty to listen. Underneath his cool, self-contained acknowledgement of the situation, he no doubt was feeling pangs of guilt and this was his way of releasing some of it. That being the case, she tilted her head obligingly to one side, prepared to listen. He wasn't to know that everything he said she would take with a hefty pinch of salt. Emily might have done a fair bit of exaggerating, but the truth doubtless lay somewhere between the two accounts.

'When Veronica died, I found myself with a teenager I didn't know and who seemed quite incapable of accepting the generous efforts made by us to smooth the path.'

'Us?' Rebecca's ears pricked up. This introduced a complete new line into the story. Had Nicholas Knight remarried? Emily had made no mention of a stepmother. In fact, she had made no mention of a woman on the scene at all, but now, thinking about it, and delving back into her memories of him, he was not the sort of man who cultivated celibacy as a chosen lifestyle.

'So she didn't mention Fiona to you?' The black eyes narrowed. He uncrossed his legs and stretched them out in front of him.

'Fiona being...your wife?'

'Fiona being my girlfriend. My dearest ex-wife rather tarnished my belief in the institution of marriage, I'm afraid.'

'No, Emily didn't mention a Fiona.'

'I'm surprised. Fiona did her utmost to get to know her.'

Rebecca thought that that manoeuvre was probably the one thing guaranteed to put off someone like Emily. She would have seen it as the threat of a mother substitute in the offing and would have instinctively reacted against it.

'Well, I'm sure that you and your girlfriend will be able to sort everything out suitably,' she said vaguely.

There was a knock on the door and Mrs Williams poked her head around it, her eyes flitting between the two of them questioningly. Rebecca smiled, relieved, but her relief lasted approximately three seconds, until he said, without the slightest hint of apology in his voice, 'We're not quite finished here. Perhaps you could give us another...'

he glanced at his watch '…half an hour?' It was just lip-service to politeness. The three of them knew that the principal would give him just as long as he wanted, and she nodded and retreated back, shutting the door behind her.

'Where were we…?' he asked, settling back to look at Rebecca.

'You were just agreeing that once you get Emily back everything will be fine. I'm sure your girlfriend will rise to the occasion and give you both all the support you need.'

'Well, now, I'm not at all sure I want to throw poor little Fiona into any such situation…' he ruminated, and Rebecca ground her teeth together in sheer frustration. She had no idea where all this was going, but she had a suspicion that it was going somewhere.

'If she loves you,' Rebecca said firmly, 'then she'd *want* to help you deal with it. And she'd also want to help Emily deal with it.'

'Oh, I'm sure she'd like nothing better than to busily try and make herself indispensable, but, you see, *I* don't want any such thing.'

'Oh, right. Well, that'll be up to the two of you to sort out between yourselves.'

'But then I'm back with my little problem, aren't I? One wayward, pregnant daughter who needs home tutoring. Even if I find the time to interview a series of prospective candidates, I'm abroad a hell of a lot, and I won't be available to supervise how things are going. And you have to admit, knowing Emily as you seem to do, that supervision is going to be essential.'

'Not if you find someone you feel confident in.'

'I'm glad you said that.' He smiled at her. The smile of a rampaging barracuda that had successfully managed to trap its prey through sheer cunning. Rebecca stared back at him blankly.

'Because *you* are going to be Emily's home tutor.' He sat back and watched her, and she could feel her face transparently revealing every single thing that was going through her head. Stunned surprise, followed swiftly by incredulity, followed even more swiftly by a complete rejection of the idea.

'I'm sorry,' she apologised, 'but there's no way that I can…'

'Why not? This is an appalling business and you yourself stated that the only way out of it for Emily, without ruining her chances in life for ever, is to employ a home tutor.' He tapped his finger. 'She trusts you, first of all.' He tapped another finger. 'You're a good teacher from all accounts, well able to get her through her exams.' He tapped a third finger. 'I won't need to supervise the situation if I know that whoever is with Emily can be trusted. So where's the problem?'

'*Where's the problem? Where's the problem?* How can you ask that?' Her voice had risen and she had leant forward, so that her bun now did the dirty on her and collapsed. With one hand she yanked her hair free and it fell around her face, straight, shiny and ludicrously image-altering. 'The *problem* is that I already have a job! Just in case it's passed you by! I can't just up sticks and take on a temporary private job because it suits you!'

'I'm not the one at stake,' he pointed out calmly. 'Emily is. If her education fails her now, then I needn't paint you a picture of what life holds in store for her.' Having said that he needn't paint a picture, he then proceeded to paint a complete and graphic picture of his daughter's supposed state of affairs, should home tutoring prove impossible for one reason or another. He, too, leant forward, resting his elbows on his thighs, and skewered her with his eyes so that she felt as though she was personally under attack.

'Suppose I do manage to find her someone to tutor her at home,' he began, making it sound as if the task would be along the lines of finding a needle, possibly even a broken one, in an enormous haystack, 'you know my daughter probably as well as I do. In fact, probably much better. She would eat the poor person alive. Or else she would do her best to ensure that the minimum of work was done, so that the duration of each tutor would be approximately a fortnight. *Which*,' he emphasised, 'would mean that any educational benefits would be eradicated.

'She would see this situation through and emerge from it well behind her peer group. With that immediate disadvantage dogging her, where would she find the impetus to suddenly pick things up and get going again? With a baby in tow? Far easier to simply let the whole damned thing slide, and in a couple of years' time, when she became utterly bored of being at home, supported by me, she would find herself some nondescript, badly paid, lowly job totally unworthy of her wasted talents.'

Rebecca felt physically besieged by his onslaught.

'Well,' she began, 'that all seems a bit on the extreme side, Mr Knight. I'm sure—'

'What *you're* sure of, at the end of the day, is that you don't want to become involved. You've uttered your little words of wisdom, but beyond that…well…' He sat back and gave an infuriatingly Gallic shrug of his shoulders.

'That's not what I'm saying at all!' she responded heatedly. How dared he imply that she didn't care? Of course she cared! And who was he to speak, anyway? Wherever the truth lay as far as his relationship with his daughter was concerned, she would bet her last pay cheque that it didn't fall on the side of Nicholas Knight, devoted father, mysteriously slandered by his only daughter. Oh, no, sir!

'Then please clarify. I'm all ears.' He cocked his head to one side and she could have hit him.

'I'm merely pointing out that I am currently employed...'

'And that's your only objection?' he asked, interested.

'It's a pretty big one from where I'm sitting,' Rebecca countered cuttingly. 'We minor members of the workforce *do* like to have a bit of job security, you know.'

There was another knock on the door.

Again Mrs Williams poked her head around and was about to speak, when he told her that they were wrapped up.

'I've just made a little proposition to your star teacher,' he opened by saying, and when the principal raised her eyebrows in polite enquiry he then proceeded to fill her in on all the details of his preposterous plan. Rebecca watched him as he spoke. He was paying no attention to her now. Every scrap of his considerable concentration was focused on the principal, who was visibly wilting from the sheer impossibility of getting a word in edgeways. He politely sidestepped every objection that began forming on her lips with the dexterity of a trapeze artist.

Finally, he informed her, as a point of passing interest, that he would compensate her hugely for releasing Rebecca immediately.

'No!' Rebecca protested hotly. 'I mean,' she carried on in a less frantic voice, 'it was just an idea that Mr Knight had. I'm sure you would be able to recommend some private tutors for Emily in the London area. Gosh, there must be thousands!'

'Yes, I'm sure—'

'No,' he cut in before the principal could finish her sentence. 'I think perhaps you both misunderstood me...' He shot Rebecca a look from under his lashes which implied that any misunderstanding was purely on the part of the principal because he had made his thoughts crystal-clear to Rebecca. 'As I explained to Miss Ryan, Emily will be an uphill task for any private tutor, apart from one who knows how to handle her, as she clearly does. I realise that it will be difficult to release her today, but the end of the term is...when? In a fortnight's time? That will give you all of the Christmas vacation to work on finding a replacement, and, as I said, I will pay generously for putting you out.'

The principal appeared to be dithering.

Rebecca could almost feel the net hanging overhead, but she wasn't going to allow herself to be trapped. She didn't like Nicholas Knight, and she especially did not want to spend months under his roof, with the past rising up inside her every time he walked into a room.

'I have a responsibility to the girls I teach,' she said carefully.

'Who, at this moment, do not require quite the same level of compassion as my daughter does. It will be a matter of a few months. Surely you can find it in yourself to spare the time?' He gave her a winning smile, and the overhead net seemed to drop a few inches closer.

'It's entirely up to you, Miss Ryan,' Mrs Williams said. 'I should be able to call upon a support teacher to cover for you until you return.'

'Yes, but...'

Two pairs of eyes focused on her, as they both waited in silence for her to complete the objection.

'It seems highly unorthodox,' she finished lamely. 'And anyway, have you considered that Emily might well disagree with the plan? She may not want to be pursued by her teacher and forced into line…'

'My daughter will just have to accept it,' he said bluntly, his mouth hardening. 'As I will make it perfectly clear when I see her. I can't unravel this situation, but I have no intention whatsoever of letting her get away with any further stupidity. She made a mistake of horrendous proportions and I shall deal with it whether she likes it or not. She's sixteen years old and she'll do as I say.'

Rebecca had visions of racks and thumbscrews and a diet of bread and water for lack of obedience. She shuddered. The man obviously knew nothing at all about teenagers, least of all teenagers like Emily. His idea of taking control of the situation had all the makings of the sort of heavy-handed attitude that could end up driving his daughter to run away.

And, however clever and cunning and unruly Emily was, she was still, underneath it all, a mixed-up child who wouldn't survive for a day on the streets of London.

The net settled over her and she sighed in defeat.

She would take the job. He was right; it would only be for a matter of months, and she would make sure that he was never reminded of any past they might have shared. She would also make sure to avoid him at all costs. She could still remember how he had made her feel all those years ago. True, she had been young and naïve then, but the man had a certain predatory charm. She might dislike him intensely, but charm had a nasty habit of getting under your skin, and that was something she would simply not allow.

'All right,' she conceded, and she saw him breathe a sigh of satisfied relief. Had he actually contemplated the possibility of refusal? If he had, then he could be an Oscar-

winning actor, because not at any point had he appeared
to doubt the persuasiveness of his arguments.

'But I shall have to discuss this with you in a great deal
more depth before I commit myself.'

'I thought you already agreed,' he pointed out. 'You
either agree or you don't agree.'

'I will work for you provided you meet my terms and
conditions.'

'Don't worry, money is no object.'

'I wasn't *talking* about money!' she snapped, suddenly
flustered at the situation she had let herself be talked into.

'Order, please!' Mrs Williams smiled at her sudden
surge of humour. 'I think it's only wise that this is discussed in some depth. I'm sure you understand that Miss
Ryan may have some misgivings, Mr Knight. But for the
moment I need use of my office. I'm seeing the governor
of the board in five minutes. Why don't you two continue
this discussion in the staffroom?'

'Why don't we continue this discussion,' he said
smoothly, rising to his feet, 'in your quarters? It'll be much
more private. The open forum can be a hotbed for gossip.'
He looked at her with the smugness of a cat that had successfully managed to catch a wily little mouse. 'We're
going to be talking about salary, despite your apparent
aversion to money, and you wouldn't want all your fellow
teachers knowing what sort of pay packet you'll be on, do
you? They might all be lining up for jobs as private tutors
in London!'

'Splendid idea!' Mrs Williams said on Rebecca's behalf,
obviously imagining a mass exodus of her teaching staff.
She walked them to the door and shook his hand, pleased
with the way things had turned out. She had anticipated
the worst and was relieved that a solution of sorts had
been found.

'But…' Rebecca began. She didn't think that she had opened so many of her sentences with 'But' in all her life.

'But nothing,' he said, steering her out of the door and smiling at the principal. 'You heard Mrs Williams.'

As soon as they were out of earshot, she turned to him and said stiffly, 'I take it you're accustomed to exploiting other people?'

'Exploiting other people?' He gave her an innocent look that didn't quite sit with his dark, raffish good looks. Rebecca thought he looked about as innocent as Lucifer on a bad day. 'I take advantage of opportunities, Miss Ryan. Perhaps I should call you Rebecca. I'm a great believer in employers being on first-name terms with their employees. Puts them at their ease.'

Rebecca, vastly ill at ease, not least because of the side-long, giggling looks she was getting from the assortment of girls drifting from one class to the other, didn't say anything.

'And I'm Nick.' He grinned to himself, as though at some private joke.

'Why does Emily not carry your surname?' Rebecca asked, leading him along corridors, past classrooms and finally into the secluded quarters of the dormitories. With no one around, she was unnervingly aware of his presence.

'Because by the time Emily was born Veronica and I were so disillusioned with one another that she did precisely what she knew would stick in my throat.'

They had reached her quarters, and she opened the door to the small but comfortable sitting room. There was just enough room for a small flowered sofa, two chairs and a couple of tables, and on either side of the fireplace bookshelves had been mounted which she had crammed with her books. He strolled over to them and began perusing the titles, while she stood and watched him, arms folded.

Did he think that this was some kind of social visit? she wondered.

'Why did you choose to live in the school?' he asked. 'Wouldn't it have been easier for a young woman like yourself to live in the town and travel in?'

'No.'

'Why not? Mind if I sit?' He sat down.

'Would you like some coffee?' She had a very small and very basic kitchen. Generally, she ate the school meals, although on her free nights she always went into the town to see her friends. It was one of the good things about working in the place she had grown up in. She had kept in touch with all her own schoolfriends and they met regularly to catch up on gossip.

'I'm fine.' His dark eyes raked over her. 'Why don't you sit down? You look very awkward towering over there.'

Thanks for the flattering description, she thought sourly. Yes, I *do* tend to tower, but there's no need to bring it to my notice.

She removed her jacket and primly sat on the chair facing him. At least she wasn't hot and stuffy now, but the blouse was still a ridiculous fit. She could feel her breasts pushing against the white material. She was also acutely aware of his eyes on her, and it seemed to her that out of the principal's office there was something rather more assessing to his gaze.

'There are a few things I want to make perfectly clear before I take up the position with you,' she began before he could launch into any more personal asides. 'Firstly, I want you to know from the start that if I am to tutor your daughter I must be given free rein to do so however I see fit. These are unusual circumstances, and sitting Emily down for formal classes as she would do in a school environment just isn't going to work.'

'And what are you suggesting here?'

'I'm suggesting that she has to feel comfortable with me if I'm to succeed in teaching her anything at all. She will have an awful lot on her mind and she will need fairly gentle handling.' He looked at her as though he disagreed with every word she had just spoken, but after a while he nodded.

'Naturally, you will want to be informed of her progress, so I suggest we arrange a time at the beginning of each week, when we can get together for a short meeting, so that I can tell you how Emily is getting along.'

'And in between these arranged…meetings…? Should we conscientiously ignore one another? Speak, but keep it to the minimum? Pretend that we're total strangers?'

'This isn't a joke, Mr Knight!'

'Nick.'

Rebecca ignored that. 'I'm sure Emily will keep you up to date with what we're doing.'

'Oh, I doubt that very much. She's managed to make herself very scarce on the occasion when she's been forced to be under the same roof as me.' His voice was bland, but she could sense emotion underlying it, and she felt a pang of sympathy. As a father, it must be difficult to realise that your only offspring would rather ignore you than include you.

'That must be very difficult for you,' Rebecca said sympathetically. 'Being denied contact with your daughter, and then, when she's a teenager, finding yourself confronted with a young woman you have never really known.'

'Thanks for the vote of sympathy.' He gave her a long, cool look and she immediately understood that private utterances along those lines were not welcome. She wondered whether his girlfriend had more access to his emotions, whether he showed her the sides of himself that he kept carefully concealed from the public gaze.

'Fine,' she said crisply. 'Now, shall we discuss the more technical aspects of this…arrangement?'

They became immersed in all the details involved, the nitty-gritty that would make up the contract of employment, which he assured her would be put in writing and sent to her for signature within the next couple of days by his secretary.

When she stood up to indicate that their meeting was now at an end, she was surprised and taken aback to find that he had remained where he was, and was staring at her in a vaguely unsettling manner. Not sexual, but somehow watchful.

'If that's all?' she prompted.

'I thought that *I* was the one doing the interviewing,' he said mildly. 'There might be one or two things I'd like to say to you.'

'Are there?'

'As a matter of fact, yes.' He linked his hands behind his head and continued to stare at her until, disconcerted, she plonked herself reluctantly back down on the chair.

'Well, fire away.'

'Firstly, I shall expect you to have meals with me— expect you *both* to have meals with me—when I'm around. I don't intend to slink through my own house like an intruder just to satisfy your bizarre preference for solitude. Admittedly, my work takes me abroad quite a bit, and my social life can be a bit disruptive as well, but there will be times when I'm around, and your presence might pave the way for a slightly smoother relationship with my daughter.'

She caught that slight edge of defensiveness in his voice

again and bit down the feeling of sympathy. Emily must be the one crack in his suit of armour which he could not hide. His feelings snaked into his voice, almost of their own accord, and he seemed unaware of it. Probably he was so accustomed to controlling people, situations, events, that he was quite wrong-footed by the one situation, the one person, over whom he had no control.

Rebecca nodded but did not commit herself to agreeing with any such plan.

'And—' he stood up, finally, taking his time and slipping on his jacket '—just one more thing…' He gave her a slow smile that made her pulses race. 'I'd just like to say that you've changed.'

Rebecca's mouth fell open.

'I know you recognise me.' He moved over to her and it was all she could do to hold her ground and not scuttle away to the side of the room in alarm. 'I could see it the minute you set eyes on me. It's been quite a while, hasn't it, Rebecca?'

Rebecca could think of nothing to say.

'Did you think that I didn't remember you? You did. I can see the answer in your eyes.' His voice was as soft and smooth as melted chocolate. It made her dizzy, a response which she immediately put down to confusion. 'You haven't got the sort of face that's easily forgotten. You look more or less the same. In fact, you seem to have aged very little over the years, but your manner's changed. If I remember correctly you were so full of life, so eager to please.'

His voice had sunk to a husky whisper, and she could feel her cheeks aflame with colour as she raised her eyes to his. Did he imagine that his syrupy charm was going to have her wilting obligingly? Or was that syrupy charm all part and parcel of his persona, something that manifested itself in every word he spoke?

'Our paths crossed years ago for a matter of a couple of weeks.'

'Why didn't you acknowledge me?'

'Why didn't you?'

He shrugged carelessly. 'I figured you had your reasons. Anyway, it was incidental to what was being discussed. After a while, I became intrigued to see whether you'd slip up, which you didn't. You still haven't lost that urge to say exactly what's on your mind, though, have you? I could see you bursting to condemn me before I'd even sat down!'

So he had known all along. She felt a complete idiot.

'Why did you run out on me all those years ago?' he asked. 'You never bothered to explain. The last I saw of you at that party was with your back turned, laughing, with a glass of champagne in your hand, and then no more contact after that. Every call I made politely declined.'

'I can't think that that's preyed on your mind all this time,' Rebecca told him, plucking every ounce of self-control at her disposal and immeasurably grateful for the fact that teaching had given her an invaluable discipline as far as her emotions went.

'Whoever said that it had?' His eyes narrowed, and not altogether pleasantly, on her. 'Although…'

'Although what?'

'I saw you there, in that room, and the past crossed my mind; it's as simple as that. And with the past came a bucketful of questions that you never answered when you decided to do your vanishing act.'

'And they won't be answered now!' she flared back at him. 'And that's another condition! I do my job, I do what

I shall be paid handsomely to do, but there's to be nothing personal between us.'

He gave her a leisurely, dangerous smile. 'I suggest you tell yourself that every morning when you wake up,' he said silkily, 'because I can feel the heat radiating from you like a furnace. If I laid a finger on you right now, I bet you'd just go up in flames. Poof! Just like that. You're even trembling, and don't bother to deny it. But still, nothing personal. At any rate, I'm involved, in case you'd forgotten.'

He stalked across to the door and stayed there for a few seconds, looking at her, his hand resting lightly on the doorknob. 'See you in a few weeks' time, Rebecca. And I don't expect you to back out because of our past little liaison. I'm sure you're grown up enough to realise that it would be a vast disfavour to my daughter if you did. For the wrong reasons.'

With that, he was gone.

CHAPTER THREE

THE station was packed. Rebecca rarely travelled down to London. Year after year, she promised herself a treat—told herself that she would vanish to London for a week or two during the summer holidays and catch up on all those exciting things a girl of her age should be enjoying: theatres, shopping, mingling with the teeming crowds, perhaps even a nightclub, if she could drag a friend down with her. Unfortunately, whenever she tallied up the prospective bill for any such jaunt, she would feel the familiar shudder of horror at the thought of spending huge sums of money to stay in a hotel for a fortnight, eat out and go to the theatre, not to mention shopping.

And the idea always evaporated. Spain for two weeks during the summer holidays was a cheaper, more reliably hotter option. And Cornwall to visit her cousin and her three boisterous children held even more appeal.

So now, with swarming crowds around her, she felt hopelessly lost, as though she had wandered accidentally into another country.

She'd managed to commandeer a trolley and she pushed it along the platform, at which point she was obliged to abandon it so that she could lug her two hefty suitcases up the escalator and out of the station.

By the time she was outside, with a freezing wind gusting around her, she felt thoroughly deflated.

This was all a horrendous mistake. She had been manoeuvred into doing something she basically didn't want to do. She had had the whole of Christmas to think about it

43

in Cornwall, and, however much she had lectured to her
cousin on what a splendid and altruistic gesture it had been
to commit herself for an indefinite period of months to a
private tutoring job, she couldn't erase the niggling unease
that had settled at the back of her mind like a heavy stone.

'Why are you looking so worried if you know you're
doing the right thing?' Beth had asked her one evening. 'I
can't really see what's bothering you. You're going to be
paid more than I could ever hope to get in a month of
Sundays, and the school is going to keep your job open
for when you return.' Which had shamed Rebecca because
Beth worked like a carthorse, looked after her three children in the absence of a husband, and rarely complained.

'I don't much like her father,' Rebecca had said, omit-
ting to mention that they had once briefly known one another several centuries ago.

'Why not?'

'He's a bit autocratic.'

Beth had shrugged. 'Humour him. Keep a low profile.
Do your job and save all the money you earn. You'll come
out smiling.' She'd grinned. 'Then you can fling it all in
my direction and buy me another car. Mine's had it.'

She looked around her now, feeling like anything but
smiling. There was a row of black cabs moving slowly
forward and a queue of people shuffling in line, waiting
their turn. His secretary had informed her that she would
be met at the station. She was on the verge of abandoning
hope, when she heard Emily's voice from behind her, and
she swung around to see her advancing gaily, confidently
and designer-clad in a black coat, black boots, with a
glimpse of jade beneath the swirling lapels.

'Sorry I'm a bit late,' she said breathlessly, and Rebecca
gave her a quick, assessing once-over. This was not the
Emily she had expected. She had expected to cope with

the teenager's ongoing despondency. Emily looked as despondent as someone who had just been told that they'd won the lottery.

'The car's parked on double yellow lines. We'll have to hurry before poor old Jason gets a ticket. The traffic wardens are terribly officious around here.' She grabbed Rebecca's arm and appeared oblivious to her attempts to move quickly with two suitcases in tow.

'So,' Rebecca finally said, catching her breath and sitting back in the plushly upholstered chauffeur-driven Jaguar, 'how are you, Emily?'

'Oh, you know.'

'If I knew, I wouldn't have asked,' Rebecca said. Without the school uniform, Emily could have passed for a girl in her early twenties. She was tall, strikingly pretty, with long black hair and very blue eyes, and with the self-assurance of someone who had learned to grow up before her time.

'Coping,' Emily said with a careless shrug. 'Glad you're here, actually. Christmas was a nightmare.' She made a face. She had been staring out of the window and she swung around to look at Rebecca. 'Most of my friends were away doing wonderful things in hot places, and I was stuck at home with Dad and that dreadful, hideous, awful woman of his. I hate her. Yuk.'

She had stopped looking like a young woman in her early twenties and reverted to teenager with an axe to grind. 'She spent the entire fortnight forcing everyone to be jolly. Thankfully, Dad was away most of the time so I only saw her now and again. When I was dragged out of my bedroom. Do you know what she gave me for a Christmas present?' Emily didn't pause to let Rebecca answer. 'A giant stuffed toy! Can you believe it? A giant stuffed panda!'

'Maybe she thought that it would come in useful for the baby.'

'I don't want to talk about that.' She had turned away again and was looking out, her shoulders hunched in defiance.

'You can't hide from it, though, can you?' Rebecca said gently.

'It's all my father talked about the whole time. My stupidity. I don't know why I had to come and live with him. He's worse than Mum. At least all she nagged me about was how much she hated him. He just nags me about everything: the clothes I wear, the way I look and my stupidity. That's when he's around. Most of the time he's not. I think he finds it easier not being around me. I get on his nerves.' There was such childish, bewildered self-pity in her voice that Rebecca felt her heart lurch. She had to remind herself that this was not about taking sides, it was about educating Emily. Her problems with her father would have to be resolved between the two of them, and possibly the panda-giving stepmother-to-be.

'I don't suppose you managed to get any work done?' Rebecca asked, changing the subject, and Emily looked at her.

'Course not. I told you, I spent most of the holiday hiding away in my room, listening to music and watching television. Anyway, I was waiting for you to arrive.'

'We'll do as much as you feel up to doing.'

'So if I can't be bothered, you won't force me?' Emily asked with adolescent optimism, and Rebecca shook her head and grinned.

'Sure I'll force you, but I'll make sure to do it gently.'

'And what if I refuse to do any at all?'

'I'll pack my bags and head back home.' The car had cleared the slow-moving traffic and was picking up a bit more speed as they headed away from the city centre to the leafy suburbs of North London.

'You can't do that,' Emily said quickly. 'You can't leave me alone with those two!'

'One of whom happens to be your father, your own flesh and blood, whether you like it or not.'

'You mean a complete stranger who doesn't like me and would rather he'd never been saddled with my presence,' Emily returned sulkily, and she then spent the remainder of the trip staring vacantly out of the window, leaving Rebecca to nurse her ongoing misgivings at what lay ahead.

On the plus side, she liked what she heard about Nick not being around a lot. At least she wouldn't have to contend with him and her suspicions that he probably remembered her as the lust-crazed teenager who had made no secret of how she had felt.

On the minus side, Emily was going to be a handful. The fact that she wouldn't discuss the pregnancy rang alarm bells in Rebecca's head. It smelled of denial, which meant that she probably hadn't dealt with the shock of the situation. Nor would she have mentally resolved the considerable consequences it entailed. She had shoved the pregnancy to the back of her mind. Did she think that by avoiding the topic it would simply go away?

She was frowning and thinking about this when Emily said, after her prolonged silence, 'Nightmare Hall approaches.'

The car turned right between two white pillars, bordered with a high, neatly clipped hedge, up a gravel path, stopping outside what was, for London, an astoundingly big house. Easily big enough for Emily to have played her hide-and-seek games over the past four and a half weeks.

'It's a seventeenth-century manor house,' Emily said in

a bored tone. 'The old man tried to fill me in on all its interesting little features when I first arrived, but he stopped when he noticed that I was yawning.'

'It's beautiful.'

'Mum and I had a ranch out in Australia.'

'Not many of those to be found in Central London,' Rebecca remarked, noticing an involuntary little grin twitch the corners of Emily's mouth.

'No. Instead we have manor houses with lots of red brick and shrubbery on the walls.' The car had slowed and virtually before it had stopped moving Emily had pushed open the car door and was hopping out. 'Don't bother trying to heave your suitcases to your bedroom,' she said brightly. 'Jason will carry them up for you.'

Rebecca glanced, embarrassed, at Jason, but instead of being offended he was smiling.

'Does the place good to have a girl in it,' he said. 'Brightens things up.'

Rebecca smiled politely, wondering how her charge would react if she heard herself being described as someone who brightened up the place.

As Emily had now vanished, she walked towards the front door and was immediately accosted by the sounds of raised voices in the hall. Unfortunately, she recognised both, and she took a deep breath and walked in.

For a split second, she absorbed her surroundings. The main hall was impressive, with highly polished wooden flooring acting as a backdrop for a huge, pale rug that appeared faded with age. To one side, an oak banister curled upwards into the upstairs quarters of the house.

Emily and her father were standing at the bottom of the staircase, Emily with her hands belligerently placed on her hips, and her father looking at her with dark disapproval.

'You *said* you weren't going to be around!' she hurled

accusingly at him, making no effort to lower her voice, and paying not a scrap of attention to Jason, who sheepishly trundled past with the two suitcases, carrying them upstairs.

'For God's sake, control yourself, Emily!' he snapped back.

Rebecca, hovering indecisively by the door, now approached them with a certain amount of grim determination. She had no intention of spending her time here in the middle of a war zone. Nothing would get done and she would emerge, at the end of her stint, a tattered bag of nerves.

'I will *not* control myself!' Hysteria was climbing into her voice, and her eyes were blazing. 'I didn't *want* to come and stay with you here in the first place! I could have stayed in Australia with my friends! You said that you were going to be away for the next fortnight!'

No wonder she had seemed so perky during the ride, Rebecca thought wryly. Emily had thought that she would have the house to herself after her enforced Christmas bonding. Now she was reacting like a spoiled brat. It was sinful to think that this child was carrying a baby, when she was little more than a baby herself.

'This is *my* house, Emily!' Nick thundered. 'I will come and go as I please and I certainly do not intend to be nagged about it by a chit of a girl!'

'But I'm *not* a girl any longer, am I?' Emily said, cunningly hitting the target spot-on. 'So it's no good treating me like one! And you can pass the message on to that horrible little tart of yours!' With which, she flounced off, leaving Rebecca to deal with a raging Nicholas Knight.

'What the hell have you teachers been doing for the past two years?' he asked her, turning his wrath on to her.

'Don't boarding-schools have a responsibility to teach basic manners to pupils?'

Rebecca drew herself up to her considerable height, thanking the good heavens that she didn't have to crane her neck up to look at him, and wishing that she could tower over him instead.

'I don't intend to have a screaming argument with you here,' she informed him with icy self-control. 'I've just spent hours on the train travelling down here, I'm tired and thirsty and in no mood to be the focus of your anger. *Do you understand me?*'

He looked at her, taken aback. 'There's no need for you to adopt that tone of voice with me,' he growled.

'There is *every* need!'

He shoved his hands in his pockets and leaned against the banister, eyes narrowed. 'Quite the rigid schoolmarm, aren't you? Those poor girls must be terrified of you!'

Rigid schoolmarm?

'Shouting and losing control of one's emotions doesn't get anyone anywhere.'

'Oh, is that right?' He gave her a slow, speculative smile which had something of the wolf about it. 'But what a dreary life if we all kept our emotions buttoned up all of the time! Wouldn't you agree?'

Rebecca wondered how they had managed to get on to the subject of her emotions when they had started out talking about his daughter. If she didn't lay her boundaries down right now, she thought, then he would walk all over her. He would not be interested in her physically, she knew that. She had known it even when he had deigned to take an interest in her all those years ago. At the time, she had been young and different. Different from the crowd he usually hung out with.

The village dance had been a novel little experience,

and even though she had been hopelessly besotted by his sophistication and glamour and sheer, abundant style she hadn't been stupid enough to allow herself to be blinded to the truth of the matter. He was out of her range. She had been the great big, jolly country girl whom he had found amusing with her big, jolly laugh and her indifference to political correctness. If she showed him the slightest crack in her armour, he would be in with a vengeance, playing his verbal cat-and-mouse games and enjoying every minute of it.

'I made it perfectly clear the last time we met that any personal references were out of bounds.'

'Mr Knight.'

'Sorry?'

'*Mr Knight.*' He grinned with indolent humour. 'I can tell from the prim set of your mouth that that qualifies as a "Mr Knight, sir" type of remark. I guess it's teaching all those girls, being in charge, being a figure of authority. Would you feel happier if I saluted you?'

'I would feel happier' Rebecca very nearly added 'Mr Knight' but she managed to restrain herself at the last minute '—if I didn't have to anticipate a battleground scenario every time you and Emily happen to be in the same room together!'

'I can assure you, you're not the only one who feels that way.' He had snapped back to the matter at hand and was staring at her with the adult version of Emily's semi-permanent sulk. It gave him a dangerous, brooding look that made her want to stare at him and look away hurriedly at the same time. Was it possible to *smell* someone's sexuality? Or was part of his sexuality the fact that he seemed so unconcerned by it?

She reminded herself that he was probably just a clever actor, and made a big show of looking at her watch.

'Coffee?' he asked dutifully. 'Or would you rather go and have a quick bath and then come down? I'm going to be here the rest of the day and this evening. Hunger should smoke my daughter out of her bedroom in due course, but while she's up there recovering from her tantrum perhaps you and I could have a little chat on how we intend to deal with her.'

'I've brought all her past school records,' Rebecca said helpfully. 'They're in one of the suitcases. I can show them to you and you can get some idea of where she's reached with her studies. She's academically very switched on.'

'So you've told me. Not switched on enough to realise that a teenage pregnancy is a waste of young life.'

He began strolling away, and Rebecca, after an internal debate as to whether she should follow him or not, hurried after him, and caught up as he was walking into the kitchen. The kitchen, she estimated, was roughly the size of her quarters at the school. One end was dominated by a large bottle-green double Aga, with a range of fitted cup-boards, and through an archway was the breakfast room, which overlooked the garden through French patio doors. It was immaculately clean. Whoever did the cooking was also extremely handy with a dishcloth.

'How do you take your coffee?' he asked, with his back to her, and when she replied he busied himself by the coffee maker, taking both mugs out to another room, where the fridge was conveniently located out of view, and re-turning to hand her her mug.

'You have a wonderful house,' she said politely, waiting for him to sit at the table and then following suit. His parents, she knew, had owned an impressive country house not far from the boarding-school. Had they owned this as well? When they had died, years ago, it had fallen to seed a bit, and then had eventually been bought and restored to an exquisite country hotel. In fact, the majority of the parents of the schoolgirls stayed there routinely at the beginning and end of each term. It did a thriving business because of its location.

'It used to belong to my parents,' he said shortly. 'When they died, I decided to move in even though it's far too big for me. They were very fond of this place.'

'I remember,' she began impulsively, then lapsed into silence.

'Remember what?'

'Nothing.' She cradled the mug between her hands. 'You were talking to me about Emily.'

'The schoolteacher hat is about to be donned, once again...?' He had pushed himself away from the table so that he could cross his legs, and she felt her eyes drawn to him, to the muscular length of his legs, much more apparent in his casual cream cords than in his suit, and to the dark hair visible where he had left the top two buttons of his shirt undone. The house was warm, warm enough for him to be wearing short sleeves. Bronzed, hard arms. She dragged her attention back to the subject of his daughter. Back to the fact that she was no longer an impressionable teenager but a hard-working teacher who had earned a great deal of respect over the years.

'The atmosphere around here is not conducive to Emily's well-being,' she said flatly, ignoring the warning glint in his eye. 'If that little episode was anything to go by, then the average civil war would count as more relaxing. She needs to have some calm around her. Try and put yourself in her position for a minute, without resorting to condemnation. She's pregnant and constantly engaging in battle with you isn't going to do anything for her stress levels.'

'I am more than happy to do my part, but—'

'Good! So do I take it that you might venture upstairs and try and make some peace with her before this evening?'

'What?' He spluttered on his coffee and sat bolt upright to glare at her.

'She would appreciate the gesture,' Rebecca said serenely.

'I am not going upstairs to try and placate a teenager…'

'*Your* teenager…'

'…who has shown not the slightest iota of civility ever since she set foot under this roof…'

'Because two years ago she was still recovering from her mother's death, only to find herself thrust into an environment she knows nothing about, with a father who finds it impossible to adjust his lifestyle to accommodate her…'

Of course he had lived his life according to his own rules. He had never had to bend to anyone. No wife, no long-term fiancée from the sound of it, no experience of children, never mind teenagers. So what if his life had been disrupted? As far as Rebecca was concerned, unless they sorted themselves out, the years would roll by and do irreparable damage. He would find himself, one day, on a road from which there would be no turning back, and any chance of trying to bridge gaps would be impossible.

'So, what happened? I'm curious.' He sipped some coffee and contemplated her over the rim of his mug. 'The more I see of you, the more I realise how much you've changed over the years. Not physically, like I said. You're just as…' He ran his eyes over her, and her mind supplied the missing words. Big. Hefty. Strapping. Robust. She had heard them all over the years. Even when they were meant in a complimentary fashion, they never failed to make her hackles rise.

'It won't work,' she snapped.

'What won't work?' he asked innocently.

'Trying to get me annoyed enough to forget about you going up to make some kind of peace with Emily.'

'Oh, for God's sake, woman, why don't you relax for a minute and stop being such a bully?'

'Me? Bully?' She gave him back his own dose of wide-eyed phony innocence, then spoilt the effect by saying, 'if I'm still sitting here in ten minutes and you're still opposite me, *then* you'll see bully!'

With which he rose from the table with an impatient, foul-humoured, theatrically loud sigh and sauntered towards the door. Rebecca followed behind him and halfway up the stairs he turned to her and said, amused, 'Think I might run off and not do as I'm told, teacher? If you had a ruler, would you be using it to slap me across the legs to get me going faster?' He grinned at the embarrassed, speechless outrage on her face, and carried on up the staircase. At the top, he paused and looked at her again, three steps behind. 'Detention if I disobey orders?' There was a wicked, amused gleam in his eyes which she refused to indulge. 'Okay.' He shrugged carelessly. 'Her bedroom is the second on the right. You can even eavesdrop if you want to make perfectly sure that I'm being a good boy.'

She fully intended to. She wouldn't have put it past him to poke his head in, mutter a few belligerent, argument-arousing phrases and then disappear down the corridor. So she remained where she was, watching as he disappeared into the room, leaving the door ajar, and then she crept until she was outside and peered through the crack in the doorjamb.

Emily was in full sulk. Sprawled on the bed with some headphones in her ears. She looked at her father as he strolled into the room, then looked away indifferently, pointedly switching up the volume on her personal stereo. She only sprang into life when he snatched it away from her and held it behind his back, watching her seethe at him from the foot of the bed.

'It's time you and I had a little chat.'

'Don't you mean *another* little chat?' Emily said, mouth turned down. She propped herself against the headboard and eyed her fingernails with the concentration of someone hoping that the apparition in front of them might vanish if they thought about it hard enough. 'Or maybe you mean another little sermon from you on the idiocy of young girls who get themselves up the stick.'

'Shut up and listen to me!' he snarled, and Rebecca fought down the temptation to intervene. If this was his interpretation of making peace, then she shuddered to think how he would wage all-out war. 'This behaviour of yours has gone on long enough...!'

'I didn't ask to be foisted on you!'

'But you were and...'

'So you admit it,' she said bitterly. 'You never wanted me!'

'That is *not* what I said.' He looked a little desperately towards the door, and Rebecca knew that he was searching for divine intervention, namely herself. Someone, *anyone*, who would interrupt the proceedings and let him off the hook. She stayed her ground. He knew that she was lurking out of sight but within earshot, she thought with a certain amount of satisfaction, but there was nothing he could do about it. If he dragged her out of her hiding place, it would be tantamount to telling his daughter that he had been forced into seeing her, and that would dismantle any hopes of a truce, however temporary. Nicholas Knight wasn't born yesterday, as he had previously told her, and neither was his daughter.

'Why are you here anyway?' she asked in a bored, sulky voice. 'Did Miss Ryan force you to come up and see me after our little argument in the hall? That would drive her nuts.'

'Don't be ridiculous. No one sent me up here to see you.'

Concealed out of sight, Rebecca grinned to herself. Getting the words out must have given him an almighty sore throat.

'She has mentioned, however, that she won't stay here if she has to put up with your lack of discipline.'

Rebecca gritted her teeth together in anger. How dared he twist what she had said to suit his own cowardly ends?

'She'd never say that. She likes me. Anyway, she can't leave me now. I told her.'

He raised his voice a little louder. 'You *told* her?' He laughed heartily, as though he had just cracked the biggest joke of his life. 'Try telling a viper to go on a starvation diet! Miss Ryan is...' he raised his voice a little louder and Rebecca clamped her jaws firmly shut just in case she was tempted to storm into the room and belt him one '...the bossiest woman on the face of the earth. She's used to *giving* orders, not *taking* them! Look at the woman: do you really think she's going to meekly listen to what you say and obey you?'

He raised his voice another notch. Any higher and Rebecca, fuming, thought that he would shatter glass. 'One glance out of those gimlet eyes and the world quakes! She's probably been known to bring grown men to their knees! She's no shrinking violet, my girl! She could probably...' his voice rose in ill-suppressed amusement '...make a flower wilt at twenty paces if she felt like it!'

'Dad, you're shouting.'

'What?' He cleared his throat and adopted a sterner

voice, but the cutting effect had gone after his momentary lapse of concentration. Emily was no longer glaring at him with adolescent belligerence. She was frankly bemused.

'Right. Yes,' he continued, 'where was I? Oh, yes, I think it's high time we tried to get along a bit better. You have a condition…'

'*Don't* start on that again!'

'I wasn't about to give you a lecture…'

'Oh, yes, you were. I can hear *lecture* in your voice before you even begin giving it…'

'Fiona's coming over to supper tonight and I expect you to be there. I don't want a repeat performance of the last time she came over!'

'She's a witch!'

'You can think what you like of her, but she makes an effort…'

'I'd rather sit in my room and stare at Ceefax than converse with your bit on the side. I'd rather count cracks on the ceiling! I'd rather write the alphabet backwards twenty times! I'd rather…' She spluttered and glared and looked childishly rebellious.

'Eight o'clock,' he said, ignoring every word of protest. 'And try to wear something appropriate.'

'You mean she disapproved of the combat gear I wore last time?' Emily asked slyly.

'Rebecca will be there, so you won't have to go it alone,' he informed her, sticking his hands in his pockets and turning to go.

'*Rebecca?* Since when are you on first-name terms with the teacher? Oh-h-h…powder-puff Fifi won't like *that*, will she, dearest Papa?' She gave just the right cackle of laughter that teenagers instinctively produced when they wanted to cause the most disruption to an adult's well-being. Nicholas, being no exception, flushed darkly at his daughter and looked as though he was on the verge of saying something hugely inappropriate, but he gathered himself together in time and walked out of the room, just managing to keep his temper in check, but shutting the door louder than was strictly necessary.

'Satisfied?' he hissed to Rebecca.

'Are *you*?'

'Oh, spare me the cheap psychobabble. Your room, while you're here and deeply tired, as you told me earlier, is on the top floor.'

'The top floor?' Rebecca glanced up at the roof and wondered whether there was some drop-ladder device she should be looking for.

'Oh, I might as well show you as I'm here.' He strode off in the opposite direction, bypassing a bewildering array of doors, and finally turned through an archway up some narrow, twisting stairs at the furthest end of the corridor. Rebecca, who could outstride the best of them, found that she was hurrying to keep pace, and almost ran into his back when he stopped at the top of the stairs and indicated where she would be staying.

It wasn't so much a room as a suite of rooms. The top floor of the house, a sprawling attic, had been converted into a bedroom, a bathroom and a large, comfortable sitting room, complete with television and video recorder. All the rooms were neatly positioned off the big central landing, and through the bedroom door she could see her suitcases waiting for her neatly on the ground at the foot of the bed.

Which reminded her...

'I overheard you say something about your girlfriend coming over this evening...'

'Blessed are those who have good hearing and listen at doors,' he said silkily, watching her flush as she remembered his less than flattering descriptions of her as ogre.

'Or maybe not. Yes, Fiona is coming over this evening for dinner. Mrs Dunne, despite being close to a hundred, is something of a cook.' He eyed her with amusement, which made her flush deepen.

'I'm big-boned,' she said defensively, folding her arms and challenging him with her eyes.

'I have no idea what you're on about. Anyway, you're expected to dine with us.'

'I'm *expected* to dine with you?'

'That's right. Eight o'clock sharp. Mrs Dunne is a stickler for punctuality. She has seizures if her food is kept waiting longer than ten seconds.'

'But…' There she went again, clinging to the ubiquitous 'But' which never seemed to get her anywhere when it came to Nicholas Knight.

'And Emily will be thoroughly disruptive if you aren't there,' he continued, pinning her to the wall with his argument.

'I didn't bring clothes for…dining in…' she said lamely.

'In that case…' He began heading for the stairs, and threw over his shoulder as an afterthought, 'Feel free not to wear any.'

'And I'm tired!' she shouted after him, furiously wondering how he had managed to arrange her life to suit his purposes and clearly had every intention of carrying on.

'Have a nap,' he replied, his voice losing volume as he negotiated the narrow steps down. 'But I'll expect you there at eight. One short train ride doesn't qualify you for jet lag.'

CHAPTER FOUR

NATURALLY, Rebecca couldn't have a nap. She couldn't have a nap because she could feel the steam coming out of her ears. She completely forgot that she was tired because she had been up since the early hours of the morning, making sure that everything was packed, and the rest neatly tidied away into two cardboard boxes which she had tucked underneath the bed.

She locked the door, wanting no more interruptions from either Emily or her father, then she set about unpacking the few items of clothing she had brought with her. Three skirts in an assortment of dark, plain colours, a few dresses which billowed rather than encased, some tracksuit pants for hanging around in, some trousers, some shirts.

She had always found shopping a problem. She was just too tall and too damned strapping to fit into all the size eights and tens which hung tantalisingly in shops and were designed for bodies like sticks. Consequently, she had always ended up buying things that fitted, but never really seemed to be the height of fashion. When the world was wearing miniskirts, she could remember stubbornly sticking to calf-length affairs that looked better with flat shoes. Tight black numbers brought on feelings of claustrophobia and her one pair of high-heeled shoes caused blisters if she wore them for longer than thirty minutes at a stretch.

In a school environment, it had never caused her a problem. As long as she looked smart and could breathe, she didn't much care how she looked. Not having to impress anyone gave her a certain sense of freedom.

When she went to visit her friends in town, she tended to jazz things up with accessories.

Now she looked at each passing garment as she stored them away, and felt more and more depressed. Black calf-length skirt. Smart but dull. Burgundy calf-length skirt, slightly flared, smart but dull. Long-sleeved woollen shift dress, smart but dull. Black trousers, smart but dull. Various jumpers, more colourful but so well used that they failed to excite. More depressing was the realisation that clothes which she would not have hesitated to wear on a perfectly legitimate date with a man now did nothing for her when she thought of wearing them to some ridiculous, meaningless dinner with Nicholas Knight and his girl-friend.

She had always been popular and she had been told, from when she was very young, that appearances didn't matter. Her mother had never once allowed her to forget that personality was everything. So she had sailed through her adolescence, tall, well built and a definite threat to any man who wanted to challenge her to a bout of arm wres-tling, with no feelings of insecurity whatsoever.

She now reminded herself of all those things and was still left with the sickening feeling that she would face Emily, her father and the panda-loving Fiona looking laughably smart. But dull.

She was seriously contemplating commandeering a pair of scissors from somewhere and turning one of the curtains into a frock, à la *The Sound of Music*, when she heard a knock on the door and Emily's voice asking whether she could come in.

Rebecca opened the door and eyed her charge in a jaun-diced fashion.

'The sound of a knock on the door, followed by your voice, does unpleasant things to my stomach, Emily. I hope you aren't here to disclose any more revelations.'

'Did Dad tell you that he's expecting us to join him and that woman this evening for dinner?'

'He mentioned something of the sort.' Rebecca stood aside to let Emily in, and watched as the girl made herself at home on the bed.

'Oh, I guess that means that he told you to be there or else face the firing squad at dawn.' She idly twirled strands of jet-black hair around her fingers. 'Likes giving orders, in case you hadn't noticed already.'

'Oh, I'd noticed, all right.' Rebecca returned to her task of packing away her clothes.

'I think he likes you,' Emily said after a while, in a dangerously ruminative voice. 'Calls you Rebecca.'

'Could that be because it's my name?' Something in the girl's tone of voice had made her ears prick up, and Rebecca continued folding her tee shirts, with her back to Emily, waiting for what else might be forthcoming.

'Yes, but it's the *way* he said it.'

'Your imagination's running away with you, Emily,' Rebecca said crisply. She had a vague idea where this was heading, and she didn't like it. The Devil worked on idle hands and if Emily was anything like her father, which she showed distinct signs of being however much she would hotly deny it, then game-playing was never far away. The teenager, aside from being in an emotionally charged situation, disliked her father's girlfriend. She was also at loggerheads with her father and had been from day one. What better game than to try and matchmake the respectable teacher with the resented father and in so doing get rid of the hated possible stepmother in the wings?

Rebecca could have told her now that she hadn't a hope

in hell. Instead, she said, changing the subject, 'Dining with your father and his fiancée—'

'*Girlfriend,*' Emily said swiftly. 'There's been no talk of marriage.' Her voice held a certain amount of nervous apprehension at that thought.

'…does leave me with a little problem of what to wear. I had planned on doing a bit of clothes shopping while I was here, but right now my cupboard is full of an array of very uninspiring clothes.'

Emily liked clothes. Despite her shows of rebellion, her items of non-school clothing at the boarding-school had all been expensive and hand-picked. Uniformly black, but statement-making black. She sat up now and walked across to the wardrobe where she did a three-second inspection of its contents and then turned to Rebecca with a cynical expression.

'I see what you mean.'

'Still, black is such a useful colour,' Rebecca said light-heartedly, pleased to have diverted the conversation away from Emily's mischievous machinations. 'And I'm about to go and have a much needed bath, so…vamoose.'

'You can always borrow something from me,' Emily said thoughtfully, one crooked finger by her mouth, head inclined to one side, and Rebecca let out a roar of genuine amusement.

'I think not!'

'Why?' Emily shot her a pained look.

'Because of that small thing known as a generation gap?'

'Doesn't mean that you have to dress in frumpy things because you're no longer a teenager.'

'Anyway, we're not the same shape,' Rebecca reminded her. 'At least not yet.'

'I don't want to talk about that.' The shutters dropped

over the blue eyes and Rebecca sighed inwardly. By her reckoning, Emily would be about seven weeks pregnant. Still early stages, but the time would swiftly approach when dodging the subject would no longer be an option.

'But you're right, we aren't the same shape,' Emily said, provoked back into the discussion. 'I have a stretchy little thing, though…'

'Not on your life,' Rebecca replied, ushering her firmly toward the door. 'Stretchy little things have never done much for me.'

'Not even when you were *my* age?' Emily asked, obviously aghast at the idea that *anyone* could go through life without Lycra.

'At your age,' Rebecca said a little wistfully, 'expensive little stretchy numbers for one-off occasions were out of our price range. I'm afraid I was rather more conventional in jeans and dungarees and weather-proof jackets that would stand the test of time.'

'Oh, right,' Emily said with such awkwardness that Rebecca smiled.

'And anyway, I *still* didn't have the figure for it then! Big bones: a woman's curse!'

Later, as she soaked in the beautifully big Victorian bath, she tried to imagine what she would look like in something small and tight. She had a vision of bulges and delicate pearl buttons popping out everywhere. It wasn't even the shape of her body. Her hair was too straight, her face was too average. She could never be sexy. Sexy, even with big bones, entailed long, curling locks, come-hither eyes and a mouth that pouted provocatively. It also entailed lots of *double-entendre* sentences left hanging half-finished and batting of mascara-laden eyelashes.

She emerged from the bath and decided that she would

be just who she was. She had never needed to impress before, and she wouldn't start now.

She brushed her hair until it shone, applied just enough make-up to feel comfortable and slipped on her calf-length burgundy skirt and an elbow-length black cardigan which fitted to the waist and was tight enough to reveal her generous bust. It would have to do. As would her flat black shoes and thick, practical tights.

Then she waited on the bed until a little after eight before making her way downstairs. *En route*, she tapped on Emily's door and discovered her to be only halfway dressed. No combat gear, but from what Rebecca could make out on the bed the outfit would hardly be twin set and pearls either.

'I'll be down in fifteen minutes,' Emily said. 'I still have to do something with my hair.'

'Well, just so long as you remember the firing squad.' They grinned at one another at this shared joke, and Rebecca descended the staircase feeling rather pleased with herself.

One of the things that had troubled her before she came was the thought of *how* exactly she should treat Emily. Handling the girls in a school environment was easy. She could be supportive without losing the necessary distance between them. She might laugh with them, but at the end of the day they knew that they were pupils and she was their teacher.

Even before she'd come to London, she'd known that that approach would not work in this instance. For a start, she would no longer be within the normal teaching environment, where school uniforms created a clear, visual barrier between the teachers and the girls. And, leaving that aside, there was the subject of Emily's pregnancy. What she would need would be a friend, a firm and supportive friend, almost as much as one who would be responsible for her educational needs. She had known, before she had stepped foot on that train, that she would have to win Emily's trust if she was to achieve anything at all, and the thought of that had been daunting.

She still wasn't there yet, but she could sense a tentative hand being held out every now and again. That shared laughter outside the bedroom had been just such a tentative hand. She knew that Emily would probably not recognise it as such, but *she* did, and she suddenly felt more confident about the whole thing.

She reached the bottom of the stairs to find that she didn't know where exactly to find Nicholas. Instinctively she headed to the kitchen, not having glimpsed much else of the house, and came face to face with the redoubtable Mrs Dunne who was busily doing things with the Aga and lots of dishes.

The kitchen smelled wonderful.

She breathed in deeply, and said the first thing that came to her head.

'This is the most magnificent smell in the world!'

Mrs Dunne, not quite the hundred that Nicholas had suggested, but certainly no spring chicken, gave her a thin, pleased smile.

'You must be the teacher.'

'Rebecca.'

'You'll be wanting Mr Knight. Back to the landing, down the corridor, second room on the right.'

'Thank you.' A woman of few words, Rebecca thought. She was easily in her late sixties, possibly even her seventies, and she wondered whether she had come with the house, the old retainer of Nicholas's parents. If he was sentimental enough to take on the house, even though it was massively big for one person, then he would easily be

sentimental enough to take on Mrs Dunne, even if he probably spent eight months of the year out of the country and
the remaining four in restaurants.

'You can tell the master that dinner will be served in
exactly thirty-five minutes, Miss Rebecca.'

Rebecca smiled and nodded. 'I'll make sure that we're
all seated and waiting,' she said warmly, liking the woman.
In her experience, people who talked too much rarely had
anything of interest to say, or what they did could be
wrapped up in a quarter of the time they took to say it.

She strode, still riding on a confident high, back through
the informal breakfast room, into the wide hall, then down
the corridor towards the second room on the right. It was
only when she was standing outside, facing a door that
was partially closed and thereby implying some sort of
privacy required within, that she felt herself falter.

She could hear voices and then the tinkling of female
laughter and her stomach clenched automatically. Her
crowd of friends she had known for years. Most of them
had been schoolfriends, with the exception of one or two
whom she had met through various academic dos which
were held in the village hall three times a year. Her social
life was cosy, if a little limited, and in no way threatening.
The last time she had felt hopelessly at a loss within a
social setting had probably been all those years ago, at that
disastrous party thrown by Nicholas, to which she had
been invited.

There, she had come face to face with the largest col-
lection of snobs she had ever met in her entire life. And
the female laughter had sounded exactly like the female
laughter which was emanating from the sitting room. She
took a deep, steadying breath and then knocked on the
door.

'Yes!'

There he went with that voice again. Was it any wonder that she constantly had to fight down the urge to call him sir?

Rebecca pushed open the door and walked in to find Nicholas and Fiona occupying the sofa. They both had drinks in their hands and looked totally at ease, sitting close to one another but not so close that they were breathing down each other's necks. Situations like this always reminded her of her own single state. She smiled politely, hovering in the region of the door until Nicholas said dryly, 'Are you going to stand there for the remainder of the evening or are you going to brave it into the witch's den?' Which brought forth another peal of amused laughter from his companion but did nothing for Rebecca aside from making her feel even more ill at ease.

'Fiona, this is Rebecca Ryan.'

A thin, elegant hand was outstretched, and Rebecca dutifully shook it, noticing the speed with which it was withdrawn. It was a hand, she thought, that was meant to be encased in a long ivory glove, possibly holding a cigarette in a jewel-encrusted holder. It was an elegant hand belonging to an elegant woman. Probably not quite as young as she would have liked to have made out, but no more than late thirties. Her blonde hair was tailored into a very short bob that curved along the jawline and her skin was porcelain-white. As if to emphasise her pallor, she was wearing a long silk ivory skirt and a camisole top, both of which heightened the look of frailty. The sort of woman that appealed to men.

'What will you have to drink?' Nicholas asked, rising from the sofa and strolling across to an exquisite piece of furniture that was apparently a drinks cabinet.

'I'll have a...' she racked her brains to think of something other than her usual white wine, because, ornamental though the bar was, it was unlikely to have an in-built chilling section '…a…'

'Oh, darling, isn't she just adorable?' Fiona crinkled her blue eyes and somehow, in those few words, managed to pull Nicholas into the same circle as herself, namely two insiders sharing the same amusement at something quaint and probably belonging to another species. 'I suppose you hard-working teachers don't have much time for the demon drink!'

'Rolling into class roaring drunk *is* frowned upon, as a matter of fact,' Rebecca said seriously, and Nicholas shot her a sideways, genuinely amused glance that escaped his girlfriend's notice. Which, Rebecca thought, was just as well, because the exquisite Fiona did not look like a woman who enjoyed her man sharing anything of himself with another woman.

'You poor darling! Now I know why I could *never* teach. Thank goodness for good old souls like yourself!'

Rebecca decided that she hated her. Was this the sort of woman who appealed to Nicholas Knight? Kittenish blondes with claws lurking beneath the well-polished fingernails?

She had edged further into the room, and perched on one of the chairs, sitting forward, her hands clasped together on her knees.

'Darling, do pour this dear a vodka and orange. You'll love it,' she said to Rebecca, implying that vodka and orange was a novel and exciting drink for women who had never touched a sip of alcohol in their lives before.

'I'll have a gin and tonic, actually.'

Fiona frowned quickly, but the shadow passed and she was smiling again, relaxed on the sofa, her blue eyes carefully inspecting Rebecca.

'Nick's told me all about poor, darling Emily,' she confided in a low, secretive voice. 'I can assu—'

'Not here, Fiona,' he said sharply, handing Rebecca the drink but remaining by her chair. 'This is neither the time nor the place for a discussion about my daughter.'

'But darling, we've got to *work together* on this one!' She winked at Rebecca, as though they were in sisterly collusion, but Rebecca flatly refused to participate in the game.

'Work together on what?' Emily's voice from the doorway sent Fiona shooting back to smile mode, and she threw her arms wide open.

'You poor, poor love. Come here!'

Emily gave her a venomous look and strolled across to the other empty chair and sat down. No wonder Nicholas had demanded her company for the evening, Rebecca thought. He, Fiona and Emily created enough invisible tension to start a spontaneous fire.

'How *are* you?' Fiona asked, no longer smiling, but now looking beautifully earnest and concerned.

'Fine. When's dinner? There's something on television I want to watch.'

'Forget it,' Nicholas grated. 'You can suffer our company tonight.'

'Oh, Nick, have a heart!' Fiona cried, and Emily glared at her. 'Let the darling do what she wants.'

'I'll stay.'

Nicholas shot Rebecca a covert look and she silently congratulated him on his tactic.

But it still made for an uncomfortable evening. The food, wonderful as it was, would have had to have hallucinogenic properties for Rebecca to miss the conflict buzzing between them. Nicholas, who fought a rearguard action to bring some normality into the conversation, was constantly wrong-footed by Emily's snideness and Fiona's sugary platitudes.

Starters were eaten in an atmosphere of simmering hostility, with Fiona attempting to edge a confession out of the teenager. By the time the prawns were cleared away by a dour Mrs Dunne, Fiona had consumed several more glasses of white wine, and was no longer disposed to be diplomatic.

'You might choose to skirt around the subject, Emily, but you do know where this leaves you, don't you?'

Rebecca groaned inwardly, not daring to look at Nicholas whose expression was growing darker by the minute.

'Up the creek without the proverbial paddle?' Emily replied flippantly. 'Why don't you concentrate on your own trivial, pointless life, Fiona, and leave me to get on with mine?'

'That is *quite* enough!' Nicholas thundered, making them both sit up, although Emily was too stubborn and Fiona, by this time, too inebriated for either to remain on good behaviour for very long.

As Rebecca desperately tried to change the subject, Fiona interrupted, closing her knife and fork on a half-finished plate of Dover sole. 'Don't you have *any* conscience? Or do you enjoy making your father's life hell?'

'I'm not making my father's life hell any more than you're making a complete fool of yourself!' Emily retorted, looking away and fiddling nervously with the cutlery.

'How dare you?' Fiona said, not managing to string her words together with much clarity. She attempted to lean forward, but ended up having to support her head in her hands.

Dessert, Rebecca thought, would be a washout, which

in turn would be a blessed relief. Fiona had clearly gone past her coherent stage and was sinking fast into green-faced silence. Had Nicholas banked on this being his girlfriend's reaction to alcohol? She was a petite woman. Drink would go to her head like incense. Had he suspected that his best ploy to get through the meal was simply to watch from the sidelines and wait for the white wine to take its inevitable toll?

She sneaked a glance at him, trying to work out what drove a man like Nicholas—gifted, sexy and insufferably clever—to a woman like Fiona who couldn't possibly pose any intellectual challenge to him.

Since the answer sprang spontaneously to mind, she decided not to pursue the question further. Clever, talented men did not necessarily see any attractions in a woman who posed an intellectual challenge. In fact, intellectual challenge in a woman probably fell soundly in the category of major disadvantage.

'Feeling all right?' Emily asked solicitously, when Fiona had waved aside Mrs Dunne's offer of some plum crumble. 'You look awful. Perhaps you'd better go home.'

'I think we'll make that the last snipe of the evening,' Nicholas told his daughter quietly, and she must have grown so accustomed to his cutting tongue that this restrained aside brought an embarrassed flush to her cheeks. 'Fiona,' he said, 'I think it's time I dropped you home.'

'I'll be fine. Just a passing headache.' Her mouth wobbled into an apprehensive smile and Rebecca could almost read the thoughts going through the other woman's head—the memory of her disintegrating behaviour.

Emily had retreated into a watchful sulk and was busy fiddling with her water goblet, staring intently at its contents.

'You have both gone to such amazing lengths to impress Miss Ryan,' he said coldly.

'I do apologise,' Fiona managed to say, although she faltered slightly on the last word, and Rebecca shook her head in embarrassment.

'Really. That's fine. It's all a stressful situation. I'm quite aware of that!'

'The wine. Far too much.' She tried to contain a yawn and failed.

'Come on,' Nicholas said, standing up abruptly and throwing Mrs Dunne off course with her round of coffee. 'It's time to break up this charming little affair.' He turned to Rebecca. 'There you are. A bird's-eye view of how we civilised human beings work when in difficult situations.'

'Will you stop referring to my situation as *difficult*?' Emily said in a high voice, and her father looked at her grimly.

'Well, one of us has to, Emily, and you don't appear to be the one. Surprising considering it's *your* situation under discussion.'

'Poor Miss Ryan!' Fiona staggered to her feet and promptly looked far greener than she had done when sitting down. 'I'm *so* sorry! What an absolute *nightmare* you've walked into! Things would be so much better if…if….' She propped herself against the table with the flat of her hands.

'If…?' Nicholas prompted coolly.

'If you'd just act more like a father!' Emily burst out in a tearful voice. 'When I came over here…I was…' With a sob, she ran out of the room, and there was stunned silence as they all listened to her fading footsteps and the distant slam of a door.

'I'll go and see what I can do,' Rebecca said quickly before the lifebelt which she had been thrown evaporated.

'No, you won't,' Nicholas told her politely, and it was only as she met his eyes that she was aware of his cold fury.

'We just never spend enough time *together*,' Fiona complained to no one in particular, in a desperate voice. 'Darling,' she pleaded, locating Nicholas across the table, 'what about if we took a holiday? I'm sure Rebecca wouldn't mind being left to her own devices for a week or so. Emily and I could...get to know one another...' She looked very doubtful as she said this, and Nicholas didn't answer. He moved around the table and grasped Fiona by the elbow.

'I'll drive you home.'

'A taxi would be fine. I've been enough of a bother already.' If she had expected Nicholas to wave down her suggestion in a chivalrous manner, then she was in for a shock, because he merely shrugged and agreed.

'Give me a minute.' He disappeared and Rebecca remained where she was, awkwardly trying to think of something to say to the unfocused Fiona.

'Do you live far away?' Weather and the road system. Thank goodness for those two dreary conversational gambits.

'Not very.' Fiona squinted in her direction. 'This is all too much for me. Emily's a little cow.'

'You have no children of your own, then, I take it,' Rebecca said heartily, glancing at the door with something close to desperation.

'No, and Emily's put me off having any for good! Nick and I were...*practically married* and then along comes that *underage bitch* and...' Her eyes were filling up, but with rage rather than sadness, Rebecca suspected.

She opened her mouth to launch into the weather option line of conversation, but was spared by the reappearance of Nicholas in the doorway.

'There'll be a taxi here in five minutes.'

'I've changed my mind, darling,' Fiona said with a bright smile that didn't go all the way in camouflaging her state of inebriation. 'I'd rather you drove me home, after all. I just want to *talk*.' She threw Rebecca another of those awful, pally smiles. 'Women's prero…proge…prerogative!'

'Too bad,' Nicholas told her coolly. 'I've already called the taxi. Come on.'

Rebecca waited awkwardly in the dining room as they walked out towards the front door. Appetites had taken a beating by the time Mrs Dunne had brought dessert, and piles of uneaten plum crumble remained on all the plates, sad, congealing reminders of how tense the evening had been.

She had no intention of ever sitting in on another hideous gathering of the sort she had just experienced. She had a responsibility to Emily, but she would have to draw lines, and unofficial objective bystander at weekly family wars was beyond the pale. If Emily had spent Christmas in an atmosphere such as she had just witnessed, then it was a wonder that the child was not in the throes of a complete nervous breakdown. Was it any surprise that she refused to acknowledge the pregnancy? That she appeared to be in a complete state of denial? She had enough on her emotional plate to cope with as it was.

She was still hovering when Nicholas reappeared in the doorway and stood there for a few seconds in silence, looking at her, then he nodded in the direction of the sitting room.

'A little chat.'

Rebecca smiled grimly at him. Oh, yes, she couldn't agree more. She followed him through, sat down and waited for him to begin.

'I apologise for this evening,' he began, and Rebecca tilted her head to one side, prepared to listen until he had run out of platitudes. However, when nothing further was forthcoming, she snapped her eyes to him and realised that he was watching her in silence, quite prepared to remain like that until she spoke.

'It was appalling,' she agreed coolly, preparing herself for the kill. 'And I'm afraid that I simply cannot put up with that sort of thing again, and nor can Emily. Whatever you and your girlfriend may think, she is still a child.'

'Ex-girlfriend.'

'I beg your pardon?'

'Ex-girlfriend. And as for the last part of your statement, yes, she *is* still a child.'

Rebecca, caught off guard by his response, looked at him open-mouthed.

'And I suppose you're wondering why I allowed the situation to develop? Having spent months attempting to intervene in their mutual, below-the-belt sniping, I decided to let it run its course on the off chance that it might just clear the air between them.' He gave a short, unpleasant laugh. 'Which it did. Fiona is incapable of dealing with my daughter, nor, I realise, would I wish her to. As for Emily…' He paused. 'She's obviously managed to some-how shove the whole question of this pregnancy under the carpet and is unable to face up to it. Has she spoken to you about it at all?'

'I've only been here a matter of a day!'

'And she's mentioned nothing. I'm right, am I not? She's managed to avoid talking about the reason you're here. Has she somehow persuaded herself that you've come here on an extended social visit, armed with a few textbooks, just for good measure? Over the past few weeks, I've put her reluctance to even mention the word ''pregnancy'' down to a natural adolescent embarrassment at discussing it with her father, whom she dislikes. I looked at her tonight. When I saw the way she wriggled away from Fiona's attempts to pin her down I realised that her avoidance of the subject wasn't to do with *me*. She just damn well can't face up to it with anyone!'

'She's afraid,' Rebecca said quietly. 'Wouldn't you be if you found yourself in a terrifying situation over which you had no control and precious few people to confide in?' If any, she added silently to herself.

'No.'

'Which is probably why you're so unsympathetic,' she retorted hotly, her cheeks burning. 'Yes, I think she's hiding from the facts, but that won't last much longer. Nature will see to that, and when she *is* obliged to acknowledge them she'll need your support.'

'Which is why I've decided that Fiona, for all her drunken ramblings, did put her finger on something.'

Rebecca's brow creased in concentration and she tried to figure out where he was heading. She realised that somewhere along the line she must have switched off to much of what Fiona had been saying. The combination of polite inanities and malicious asides had turned her stomach to the point where it had been easier simply not to listen. Her attempts to make the peace, initially, had been as futile as trying to fight two swordsmen with a toothpick, and in the end she had simply allowed herself to float downstream in her own thoughts.

'What?' Rebecca asked eventually.

'It's time Emily and I got to know one another a little better.'

Rebecca breathed a sigh of relief. He had seemed so intransigent at the beginning that she was a little surprised at the suddenness of his decision. Surprised but pleased.

He would probably make more of an effort to arrive home from work earlier in the evenings, and of course, if he was determined to acquaint himself with his daughter, then she, Rebecca, would not find it difficult to vanish as appropriate and give them both space and time to be together.

She rapidly worked out that it could not be better as far as she was concerned. Nicholas Knight made her nervous and she could think of nothing better than having the perfect excuse to avoid his company. She didn't care for the way his presence made her thoughts travel down the disturbingly fragile route of evaluating all her past boyfriends and finding them wanting.

'I couldn't have hoped for anything better!' she said with genuine warmth.

'Good!' Miraculously his rage seemed to have disappeared. 'Because I shall be taking a month off. Emily and I will get to know one another somewhere small, private and without distractions…and you're coming along for the ride!'

CHAPTER FIVE

'WHAT?' She looked at him frankly aghast.

'I said—' he began in a laborious voice, and she interrupted him before he could repeat himself.

'Yes, yes, yes. I *heard* what you said. I'm just a little…taken aback, that's all.' *Taken aback?* Her heart was hammering like a steam engine in her chest!

'Why?'

'*Why? Why?* Isn't it obvious?'

'No, as a matter of fact,' he told her, narrowing his eyes ominously. 'I would have thought that this was the ideal solution. Correct me if I'm wrong, but haven't you made it clear from the start that you blame all of my daughter's bad behaviour on me?'

'Not *all*, no.'

'Well, thank you for that small crumb of support.' He sighed and ran his fingers through his hair. 'And maybe you've had a point,' he conceded graciously. 'When Emily arrived here, I was hardly the most compassionate father in the world. Apart from the blood bond, we were complete strangers. She was suspicious and resentful of me, and I just never seemed to have the time to devote to her. I was busy running my life and slowing down to accommodate a sullen teenager was…difficult. And, before you barge in with accusations of deliberate neglect, Emily was never neglected. She had money at her disposal and I suppose I made the classic mistake of assuming that money equated with time, which it doesn't.'

'So you've now decided that you're going to put that

right? Why now? Why not six months ago? Or a year ago? Why *now*?' Her throat was feeling restricted. Her breathing was shallow. Her skin was burning. She was going through the classic symptoms of panic, and she fought them down, because she wasn't quite sure why his suggestion should throw her into such a state of turmoil and *not knowing* filled her with even more alarm.

'Because circumstances have forced me to,' he said bluntly. 'Emily's pregnant and, however disgusted I am with that particular situation, there's no point in hiding from it. Like I said to you, she's obviously in denial about the whole thing. She won't discuss it, she won't even allow the subject to be broached, and it's time...' He shrugged but his eyes slipped away from hers, and she could sense an admission of guilt there—guilt that his attitude might have contributed to Emily's lack of control, guilt that he had not spotted the danger signals when he should have, guilt that he had been given the chance to redeem himself in his daughter's eyes and he had failed.

'It's time we got to know one another and she realised that she can...trust me.' He spoke heavily, as though the entire concept was almost too big to absorb. 'If I stay here and try to fit her in with my work schedule, then there's no chance of that happening, even with all the best intentions in the world. It's impossible for me to have any kind of normal routine here. Work is just too intrusive. If I'm away, then I'm less inclined to find my time interrupted by faxes and phone calls and meetings and trips abroad.' He gave her a long, unflinching look. 'Schoolteachers lead very ordered lives. Classes are conducted during the day, and at five your time is your own.'

'Not quite,' Rebecca informed him, but she could see his point. Where did his working time begin and end? His life had always been his work, she assumed, and trying to create a split now would be almost impossible.

'As good as,' he rebutted flatly. 'Anyway, the way I see it, you can bring all the textbooks over and you can still spend part of the day teaching her…in more relaxed surroundings.'

More relaxed surroundings? How could her surroundings be more relaxed if Nicholas Knight was going to be around, hovering and waiting to spend quality time with his daughter, and, by association, with *her*?

'How can you not avoid work over here, and then just up and leave for a month?'

'Oh, I shall communicate with my people. Voice mail and e-mail and fax machines and laptop computers. Wonderful inventions. But I shall be able to switch the lot off at will.' He was throwing her one of those speculative looks again. 'So does it all make crystal-clear sense to you now? Or do you have any more objections?'

'I don't have any *objections*,' Rebecca said dubiously.

'You wouldn't have thought that judging from the expression on your face.' He allowed a few seconds of silence to drip between them. 'Unless, of course, there are other reasons why you're so hesitant about the idea…'

Rebecca flushed but didn't say anything.

'Personal reasons, perhaps?' he asked smoothly.

'Personal reasons?' She knew that she shouldn't ask, but she did anyway. 'Such as what?'

'Such as the fact that we're not complete strangers to one another? Such as the fact that you were once infatuated with me? Such as the fact that I might make you nervous?'

'That's ridiculous!'

'Is it? Then why is it that you act like a cat on a hot tin roof whenever I'm around? And don't try and deny it. We may not have known one another for very long, but from what I remember guile was never something you excelled in.'

'You wouldn't know *what* I excelled in!' she flared. 'We were two people from such different worlds that we might as well have come from completely different planets.'

'Is that why you disappeared without explanation?' he inserted quickly. 'Because you got scared about our social differences? Did you think that they mattered to me?'

'This has nothing to do with Emily, with why I'm here…'

'It has *everything* to do with Emily. If you have a problem with me, then you might as well tell me now and we can do something about it.'

'Like what?' Rebecca asked curiously. 'I *don't* have a problem with you, just for the record. Any feelings I had for you—and I don't even remember what they were—are in the past, but if it had been different, tell me, what would you have done about it? Do you think that you can sort everything out? Even other people's emotional frames of mind?' She gave a short, sarcastic laugh. 'You've already admitted that you failed to rise to the occasion with your daughter! You might be able to snap your fingers and get what you want as far as work goes, but *real life* doesn't work like that. You can't just snap your fingers and—lo and behold!—other people's untidy lives are sorted out *because you so decree*!'

What a time to remember how he had made her feel! What an awful time to remember her nervous, heady excitement when she'd realised that he was interested in her! He had made her laugh the way no one had before, or since for that matter. He had been witty and charming and powerful and in the space of a couple of days she had fallen for him hook, line and sinker. All the boys of her own age had suddenly seemed puerile in comparison.

Nicholas Knight had filled her with a raging, burning passion and even though common sense had won the day the memory of him had lingered in her head a lot longer than she would ever have admitted.

It seemed horribly unfair that she should have put him behind her, only to run slap-bang into her past just when she least expected it.

'*Real life?* What do you mean by *real life*? Are you telling me that because I'm wealthy I somehow don't know what real life is?' Now it was his turn to give a snort of disbelieving laughter. 'Is your life any more real than mine? If you ask me, it's less so. I mean, why are you hiding away in a boarding-school?'

'I am not hiding away in a boarding-school!' Rebecca responded furiously.

'No? Then what are you doing there? Aren't house mothers or whatever they're called supposed to be matronly spinsters who don't mind relinquishing their privacy for the higher purpose of looking after schoolgirls? What are *you* doing there?'

She could feel the blood rush to her hairline.

'I didn't have much choice, as it happens!' she snapped back at him. 'I had only just started teaching at the school when Mum died and I had nowhere to go! We lived in a council house and I was thrilled when the school approached me with the offer of free accommodation! It was never my intention to remain as a house mother there indefinitely, until I became covered in cobwebs! I've been saving like crazy for a down payment on a place of my own, and by next year I should have enough! I have *never* been cushioned by money. I've worked damned hard for everything I have, and I don't appreciate you implying...'

'I'm not implying anything. But just because your circumstances were more reduced than mine that doesn't necessarily make you a better human being.'

'I never implied that it did.' She was beginning to simmer down but she could still feel shards of anger running through her. How they had reached this point in the conversation was beyond her.

'Good! So that's all settled, then.' He gave a brooding half smile, as though whatever reaction he had managed to prod out of her had been precisely the reaction he had been hoping for. 'You have no personal hang-ups about me and you're dying to put my little proposal to the test.'

The man, she thought, dazed, moved faster than the speed of light. By getting her on to the emotional fast track, he had succeeded in shooting down all her potential objections to his idea.

'What if Emily doesn't want to go?' Rebecca pointed out, maliciously keen to put a dent in that supreme self-confidence of his. 'She might dig her heels in. She's in a pretty unstable state at the moment and she might just want to cling to what she's familiar with.'

'In that case, we'll have to make sure that we're *very positive* about the whole idea, won't we?' he said softly and with an undercurrent of menace in his voice. 'I know that I can count on you to do that.'

'I'll try my very best,' Rebecca said in a saccharine voice. 'But she may not be over the moon at the thought of enforced time with just the two of us, a stack of textbooks and no outside diversion.'

'Oh, with a little persuasion, I think she might come round to the idea,' he drawled. 'Especially if there's the promise of some better weather. Don't forget, Emily's not used to cold winters. I personally think she'll be overjoyed at the prospect of a month in the sunshine somewhere. And as for being cooped up with the two of us, well, I often

find that comparison works when trying to convince someone of something. You can tell her that if she's reluctant
to spend time with just the two of us, then imagine if Fiona
had been included in the equation as well. That should see
her packing her bags straight away!'

'Isn't that emotional manipulation?'

'Is it?' He gave her an innocent look. 'Mm. Maybe
you're right. Well, you'll just have to use that imagination
of yours.'

'And when were you thinking of leaving?' Rebecca
asked, glumly acknowledging that all points of exit were
now blocked.

'Soon. Emily hasn't mentioned the pregnancy once, not
even when I've attempted to raise the subject. She's just
flounced out of the room. But by my calculations she's
only—what?—two months pregnant? She's got another
month or so before she's going to have to start seeing
doctors or whatever. Which leaves us a clear month to
work on her.'

'To *work on her*? You make it sound as though she's a
project. I hope you don't intend to see her as one. A project
to get up and running and then promptly abandon once
you feel you've put in the required effort.'

'Oh, for God's sake, stop pulling everything I say to
pieces, Rebecca.'

The shock of hearing him call her by her first name
made her blush, a silly, childish reaction that made her feel
unreasonably annoyed with herself.

'I'm being a realist,' she told him stiffly. 'It comes with
the job.'

'I'm suitably chastised, in that case,' he said in an un-
repentant voice. 'I shall leave it to you to inform Emily of
our plans.'

Our plans? Rebecca thought sourly. Just like him to

twist everything round to suit himself. They both knew that Emily would receive the idea like a dose of flu and by sharing the blame he would be doubling the impact.

He stood up, stretched and glanced at his watch. When he stretched, a tiny piece of shirt that had been tucked into the waistband of his trousers escaped, revealing a sliver of hard, masculine torso from which she hurriedly averted her eyes. He had never been her lover, in the full sense of the word, but she burned with shame now to remember how she had used the image of him to stoke her fantasies when she'd finally lost her virginity to another man at the age of twenty.

'Good Lord!' he exclaimed. 'Is that the time? Do you realise that it's after midnight?' He gave her a wicked grin. 'I hope you don't turn into a pumpkin after twelve?'

'Not unless I miss my medication,' Rebecca said coldly, not much caring for what she thought was a definite smirk in his voice. She stood up and smoothed down her skirt, which looked every bit as dull as she had anticipated it would.

'And you might need to get a few more clothes,' he said casually, and she raised her eyes to find him staring at her. 'I doubt whether smart, neat clothes will be called for if we go somewhere hot on holiday. Did you bring anything a little less...formal?'

He was trying not to grin but he obviously couldn't keep a straight face and she could quite willingly have whacked him across the head. Female she might be, but delicate she most certainly was not, and a whack from her would have sent him flying. Or at least made him lose his balance, on *all* fronts.

'I didn't pack my floral shirts and shorts,' she told him in a voice laced with sarcasm, 'not having foreseen a hot holiday immediately upon my arrival. I suppose I should have thought of it!'

'You certainly can't go wrong by anticipating things! Anyway, as far as timing goes, I shall have to wrap up a few things here before I leave, but I think we should be ready to set sail in a week's time.' He raised his eyebrows as though waiting for her to object. 'I shall get my secretary to work on a few places…and contacts. Any suggestions?'

'No. None.' She was tempted to inform him that extensive travelling had never been part of her agenda, but resisted the impulse.

'And by the way,' he said, as she began heading for the door, 'I shall cover the cost of whatever clothes you buy.' He held up his hand before she could open her mouth to protest. 'And don't even try arguing the point. The money will be in your bank account by lunchtime tomorrow.'

Which took neat care of that objection, even if she had had the foresight to consider it, which she hadn't.

She spent a restless, fractured night. It was as if her subconscious had suddenly been set free, to go on its merry way, and her dreams were punctuated with strangely erotic images of Nicholas Knight. He had liked her size, had said it turned him on to feel someone substantial beneath his hands. In her dreams, he didn't just touch her breasts and she was no longer the prurient teenager who had struggled to maintain control. Between the hours of three and six in the morning, she had allowed him full access to her burning body, revelling in his sensuous, lingering, minute exploration.

She awoke awash with mortification and made very sure not to step foot outside her bedroom until she was pretty certain that he would have left for work. Even then she found herself, primly attired in her dark skirt and white blouse, tiptoeing out of her bedroom and glancing nervously around just in case. Just in case he pounced out from behind something and somehow managed to glean from her expression exactly where her errant mind had spent the past few hours travelling.

She only relaxed when she was in the kitchen, where she found Emily, in a pair of jeans and a sloppy jumper, sitting in front of a bowl of cereal and the gossip page of a tabloid.

'Didn't I tell you that the woman was awful?' were her opening words. 'There's bread and cereal, by the way. Elsie's busy somewhere in the house, doing cleaning things.'

'Elsie?'

'Mrs Dunne, the formidable housekeeper.'

Rebecca helped herself to some coffee and sat down opposite Emily.

'So?' Emily prodded, shoving her empty bowl away and casting a few last, lingering looks at the 'Saucy Susie's Secret Wedding' headline glaring out from the newspaper. 'Admit it, she's even worse than you imagined.'

'I presume you're talking about Fiona.'

'Aren't you going to have anything to eat?'

'I don't normally eat breakfast. I just grab a cup of coffee.'

'That's very unhealthy,' Emily reprimanded her. 'As a teacher, you should know something about nutrition. Breakfast is the most important meal of the day, followed by lunch, and dinner should just be something light.'

'I'll remind my stomach tomorrow,' Rebecca promised. Despite the late night and hormones which should have had her looking exhausted and stressed, Emily presented a picture of glowing good health. Her hair hung down past her face like a black curtain, her skin was pink and there was not the slightest hint of baby to be glimpsed from her slender frame.

'She's disgusting,' Emily said, carrying on the conversation with which she had initially greeted Rebecca. 'I hated her the minute I first laid eyes on her. How could my father see *anything* in a woman like that? How *could* he? Do you know that the first thing she suggested when I came over here two years ago was that I should be sent to a boarding-school? Oh, she wrapped it up in all sorts of flowery words but the bottom line was that she didn't want me around. Dad's away a lot and she just didn't want me around cramping her style when he *was* here. She's as hard as nails underneath all of that sugary coating. Did you see that?' Two bright patches of colour had surfaced on her cheeks. 'I could kick myself for storming out like that last night. She must have had a field day gloating.'

Rebecca sipped her coffee and thought that a field day was probably the very last sort of day Fiona was having just at this moment in time.

'Things would have been different if *she* hadn't been around. Dad might have...' She lowered her eyes and stared mutinously at the folded newspaper in front of her.

An adolescent's emotional grappling locked inside the body of a beautiful woman. Emily played at being a cool, sarcastic adult but at moments like this it was very easy to see just how young she was. Right now she looked as though she was fighting against tears.

'She wants me out of my father's life for good,' Emily muttered bitterly, and Rebecca sighed.

'Isn't that a bit of an exaggeration?' she asked mildly. 'Perhaps there's just a simple personality clash...' Not that it mattered now.

'She wants to stick me in a boarding-school and when

I'm done there she'll probably arrange a university some- where a million miles away.'

Why was Emily talking as though there wasn't the small matter of a pregnancy scuppering all those plans, if indeed those had been Fiona's plans at all? Denial. Again. Nicholas had been right. Undiluted time with his daughter was the only way for them to sort out some pretty basic problems.

'Your father and I had a little chat last night after you'd gone to bed.'

'Was that woman there?'

'No.'

A shadow of relief crossed Emily's exquisite face.

'One of the things Fiona suggested after you'd gone was a holiday somewhere…'

'No!' Her head jerked up and she had clenched her fists into tight balls. 'I am *not* going on holiday anywhere with that poisoned dwarf!'

'Calm down!' Rebecca commanded, in her best teacher's voice. 'And leave Fiona out of the equation.'

'How can I?'

Rebecca, caught on the horns of a dilemma, decided to take the plunge. Ideally, Nicholas should have been the one to communicate with his daughter that his relationship with Fiona was finished, but since Rebecca could imagine him doing no such thing she cleared her throat and said neutrally, 'Because she will no longer be a part of your life. I gather your father has ended the relationship.'

Emily's expression, the down-turned, truculent mouth, held disbelief, then very slowly she began to smile. It was like seeing the promise of sun behind a bank of thunderous clouds.

'He's *ended the relationship*? Are you sure? What did he say? Precisely? Did he say "I've ended the relationship''? Did you overhear him telling Fiona that? What did *she* say?' Emily gave a hoot of laughter. 'All that simpering for nothing! What a scream! I wish I'd been a fly on the wall!'

'I didn't overhear anything,' Rebecca said firmly. 'I don't make it a habit to eavesdrop with a glass to the wall. Your father simply told me that their affair was finished.'

'I won!'

'This isn't a game, Emily!' Rebecca said sharply, wondering how she could be so overwhelmed by this item of news, when far more overwhelming things were lurking on the not-too-distant horizon. 'And, as I was saying, before…before Fiona left, she mentioned that a holiday might have been an idea.'

'With my father?' Her mouth curved into lines of scathing disbelief. 'I don't think my father's ever had a holiday in his life before. He certainly hasn't had one since *I've* been around. The only thing he cares about is his work.'

Here we go again, Rebecca thought. Goodbye, Fiona-induced tantrums, hello, father-induced ones.

'He's going to take some time off.'

'Yeah? How much? An hour and a half? Between meetings?' She gave a very adult snort of incredulity.

'A month,' Rebecca announced calmly, watching with some satisfaction as Emily's eyes opened like saucers.

'*A month?*' she squeaked. 'Are you sure about that? Are you sure he didn't say *a day*?' When Rebecca shook her head, Emily burst out with nervous hostility, 'I can't go on holiday for a month with him! What am I going to talk about? I've barely had a conversation of longer than ten minutes with him in all the time I've been over here!' She was beginning to look panicked and horrified. Rebecca felt she could identify with that particular feeling.

'It's a stupid idea!'

'Are you scared?' Rebecca asked gently.

'Scared of what?'

'Of the possibility that you might actually get to know your father?'

'I don't *want* to get to know him!'

'Then why did you care so much that Fiona was trying to wedge herself between the two of you?'

Emily looked staggered by this piece of simple logic. 'I just didn't like the woman,' she said stubbornly. 'Anyway, I can't go. I have to stay here and study.'

'Oh, there'll be no end of that,' Rebecca said brightly. 'I shall make sure that I bring along all the textbooks we'll need.' She never would have thought that she might end up siding with Nicholas on this ridiculous plan, but she had. Somehow she had found herself forming an invisible united front with him, even though her own feelings on being in Nicholas's company twenty-four hours a day mirrored Emily's.

Emily threw her a cornered look. 'But…'

'No buts.'

'Where, then?' she asked in a defeated voice. 'Somewhere hot, I hope. Then I can at least spend my time sunbathing. I hate the weather over here. It never even has the decency to snow in winter. Just rain and cold and more rain. I lived on the beach in Australia.'

'France,' Rebecca said, thinking on her feet, and Emily made a face, as though the prospect of a month in France was roughly about as inviting as a month of hard labour. 'Apart from your studies, you can practise your French.'

'Why?'

'Because that's why I'm here, or have you forgotten the little matter of your pregnancy?'

Down came the shutters, and she lithely unfolded herself from the chair and headed towards the kitchen sink, where she made an enormous clatter washing up the few things that had been lying on the counter. To top the noise levels, she began humming to herself. Good job there wasn't a vacuum cleaner handy, Rebecca thought, or she would have switched that on and let it run if only to drown out the possibility of the discussion being prolonged.

'So today,' Rebecca said, sneaking up on her and speaking into her left ear, 'is a free day, Emily. I shall have to do a spot of shopping, but don't think that you can while away the hours in front of the television. I came with a few prepared exercises for you. You'll find a geometry paper on my dressing table and I'm sure I'll return later today to find that it's been done.'

'Or else?' Emily raised one insolent eyebrow.

'Or else...nothing.' Rebecca shrugged. 'Your future is the one under the microscope here. I can help you, but only if you're prepared to help yourself, and if you aren't I shall be very disappointed but there will be absolutely nothing I can do to remedy the situation. I can't lock you in a room and force you to work. You're not a child, Emily, and whilst I may be able to support you and motivate you you've got a responsibility to yourself as well. You've got to motivate yourself to work. You've got to think ahead to after the—'

'Don't say it!' Emily flashed, then she licked her lips nervously. 'Okay. I like geometry anyway. What time will you be back?'

'This afternoon.' She wanted to see Nicholas first, to tell him that there had been a slight change of plan as to their destination. She didn't want to find that complicated arrangements had been made for a month of undiluted, distracting sunshine.

She knew where his office was from her communications with his secretary and within an hour she was standing inside Reception, taken aback by the size of the building and dazed by all the glass and large potted plants which seemed to give it a vast greenhouse aspect.

This, she thought, was a situation where her size came into its own. She looked authoritative. She had worn a smart suit and she strode purposefully to the circular desk in the middle of the room and informed the small, pretty brunette behind it that she wished to leave a message for Nicholas Knight.

'Nicholas Knight?' The girl's expression subtly altered and her eyes were curious. 'Is he expecting you?'

'No, he's not. But I don't want to *see* him. I just want to leave a message with his secretary.'

'Of course. I'll just get through to his secretary and inform her that you're on your way up. Your name...?'

Five minutes later, Rebecca was riding the lift to the seventh floor. She stepped into the plush, respectfully silent atmosphere of a floor dedicated to top executives. The differences between this place and the school staffroom couldn't have been more pronounced. It was not open plan. The central area comprised two desks, where two identically blonde secretaries of indeterminate age sat behind computer terminals and telephones. And, of course, there was the usual array of perfectly manicured plants. Rebecca deduced that someone in the decision-making ranks had a horticultural interest.

She was directed to the last door on the left and was at a bit of a loss when she purposefully strode in to find that his secretary was not at her desk but his office door was open and she could see him, on the telephone, talking and at the same time frowning at whatever was on the computer screen in front of him.

He signalled for her to come in and she sighed with frustration. She had banked on leaving a message. She hadn't psyched herself up for having a conversation with him.

'Right,' he said once she had sat down on the chair facing him. 'What can I do for you?'

'I didn't come to see *you* actually. I came to leave a message for you.'

'One that couldn't wait?'

'I wouldn't have made this trip here if it was something that could have waited, would I?' she said politely, and she saw a shadow of amusement cross his face. It seemed his instinctive reaction to her every time she adopted her teacher's voice. She had never been a source of amusement to any man before and she wasn't too sure whether she liked the sensation. 'It's about this trip you've planned.'

'What about it? Don't tell me that Emily's digging her heels in, because if she is then she'll just have to un-dig them.'

'Naturally she wasn't overjoyed at the suggestion,' Rebecca told him, not moving straight to the point as she had planned. 'In fact, she was a bit alarmed at the thought of being cooped up with you for weeks on end.'

'Oh, well, that does a hell of a lot for me!' he grated with an angry wave of his hand. He sat back in the leather chair and pushed himself slightly away from the desk. 'You're telling me that you trekked halfway across London to bring me that little titbit?' The phone rang and he snatched it up and barked, *'Yes!'* down the receiver to whoever had had the folly to telephone at that precise moment in time. A few clipped words and he slammed the receiver down and muttered something under his breath.

'I can't win, can I?' he snapped, before she could interrupt. 'Either I'm absent and she complains or I'm present and she complains. I get the impression that Emily just likes *complaining*. She gets expelled from school for being pregnant and instead of trying to be accommodating, which is the road any *normal* girl would go down, she just carries on as though nothing's happened!'

'Finished?' Rebecca asked, tilting her head to one side and making full use of her teacher's voice again.

'And don't give me that businesslike little tone of yours, either! You keep forgetting that I know Rebecca Ryan when she isn't wearing her schoolmarm hat!'

Rebecca went bright pink. Blushing had always struck her as such a *girlie* thing to do, and she was so *un-girlie* that it made her feel ridiculous, but Nicholas Knight just had a curious knack of throwing her into a state of embarrassing confusion.

'I was *going* to say,' she informed him in a well-modulated, controlled voice which she hoped was more or less matched to her expression, 'that, despite her misgivings, she's agreed to the idea. But the reason I came down here was to stop you from booking anywhere hot and relaxing.'

'What? Why?'

'Because I thought about hot and relaxing and I came to the conclusion that those were two things that wouldn't go a long way to getting your daughter to put her head down, study and take stock of her situation.'

'So…?'

'So I've decided that the best place would be France. She can use her French and she won't be tempted to spend all her time sunbathing. Not unless she's attracted to the idea of hypothermia.'

'*You've* decided on France?'

'That's right.' Now that she had said what she wanted to say, she stood up and immediately felt a lift in her self-confidence as she towered over him at the desk. It didn't last for very long. He stood up as well and she was back

to having to look up at him. 'Is there a problem with that?
I came here because I didn't want you to arrange anything
and then have to rearrange it.'

'What makes you think that I would have *rearranged*
my plans because you said so?' he asked silkily, and she
felt another wave of colour flood her face. After a few
moments of enjoyment at her expense, he shrugged.
'France it is. I'll get it arranged today. Now, where are
you off to?'

'Shopping,' Rebecca said indistinctly. 'But I've left
work for Emily to do.'

'And then?'

'Back to the house.' He had moved closer to her and
her nervous system was not co-operating with her brain.
In fact, it was going into overdrive.

'I'm off to a meeting now, but meet me for lunch in…'
he looked at his watch '…two hours. San Antonio's just
off Covent Garden.'

'Lunch? What for?' she asked, dismayed.

'So that I can seduce you,' he murmured in a velvety
voice, and shock made her mouth drop open. He grinned
at her. 'Alternatively, if that plan doesn't grab you, then
we can discuss how we're going to organise this holiday
so that I return to England with a daughter who's faced
up to her situation and is capable of conversing with me
for longer than three seconds at a stretch without flouncing
off.'

Rebecca closed her mouth, and he gave her a sexy,
charming smile. 'Unless you prefer the seduction option?'

While her legs were still capable of supporting her, she
fled from the office with an ignominious lack of authoritative control and sought refuge in the therapeutic remedy
of shopping.

CHAPTER SIX

SHE bought wildly. Or at least wildly by her definition. By the time twelve-thirty rolled around, she had managed to accumulate what felt like her body weight in bags and stepping into a taxi to take her to the restaurant was bliss. Her arms were aching, her feet were blistered because she had stupidly gone to his office in shoes she was unaccustomed to wearing and she could feel the first stirrings of a headache.

If he didn't show up within three minutes, she was not waiting for him.

He was there and waiting, and she was shown to their table where he took one look at the assortment of shopping bags and didn't bother to hide his mirth.

'Shopping. The one thing in life you women do best.'

'Ha, ha,' Rebecca said, glancing around her for somewhere to put the wretched bags. 'Haven't those sexist notions been put to bed in this day and age? I need somewhere to put all these bags.'

He signalled for a waiter. 'The lady needs somewhere for her shopping,' he said, still grinning broadly, and the waiter grinned back at him in shared understanding.

'Perhaps another chair?' she asked politely. Her feet seemed to have expanded three sizes within her shoes and if she didn't sit down quickly and slip them off she feared that she might never walk again on account of the blisters on her heels.

'I would be happy to store them for you,' the waiter said, 'and I could also relieve you of your coat.'

'Could you relieve me of my feet as well?' Rebecca asked, straight-faced, and she heard the sound of choked laughter from Nicholas's area. 'The bags and coat will be fine. Perfect, in fact.' She slipped out of her coat, handed over her five-ton burden and sat down with a sigh of relief.

'What on earth have you bought?' he asked, sitting back and watching her as she perused the menu that had been placed in front of her. She could feel his eyes on her and with a twinge of irritation she realised that she had had no time to do anything about her face. She doubted that there was any lipstick left on her lips, her hair had been blown by the wind into a challenging tangle of brown and her cheeks, she knew, would be boasting that healthy pink look that was fine in the country but not quite so appealing in a smart London restaurant.

'Two pairs of trousers, two jumpers, two pairs of shoes, three long-sleeved thermal vests to wear underneath the two jumpers and some socks.' She looked up from the menu and caught his eyes. 'It's the most shopping I've ever done in one fell swoop in my entire life and I hope never to repeat the exercise.'

'You mean you *don't like shopping*?' he asked with a horrified grin. 'You're a woman and you *don't like shopping*?' He drank some of his mineral water and continued to survey her with that aggravating expression of amusement that she found unnerving and unsettling at the same time.

'It's a crime, I know. Lock me up.' She returned her attention to the menu, which was infinitely less destabilising than the man sitting opposite her, and was relieved when the waiter returned to take their order. They were both going to have the salmon, with salad for starters. Trying on clothes in those changing rooms with the fluorescent lights that could turn Helen of Troy into a hag had convinced her that she needed to do something about her weight. She was a big girl, but seeing herself in so many full-length mirrors in the space of a morning had shown her that she could do with a little streamlining.

'Well, *you* try being my size and finding something that looks reasonable,' she told him irritably.

'I know.' He shook his head ruefully. 'It's such a chore. Frocks just don't look right on me either. My size as well. Nowhere seems to cater for anyone over six foot.'

Rebecca felt her mouth twitch.

'There,' he said with satisfaction. 'That's better. The lady can smile even though her arms and legs are aching.' He sat back so that his starter could be placed in front of him, not taking his eyes off her face. She took a rapid and dizzying trip down memory lane to when she was younger and was willing to let herself melt at that very same smile that held such wit and humour.

Fortunately common sense kicked into gear and she yanked herself back to the present. Lunch with a man who operated in a different world from her, so that they could discuss his daughter.

'I left Emily with work to do,' she said crisply, tucking into her salad and refusing the offer of wine.

'And did she jump at the chance?'

'*Jump* is a bit of an exaggeration. *Reluctantly stagger towards* might be more appropriate, but it's better than nothing. At least that indicates that somewhere inside she still sees the need for an education and she's prepared to take it in her stride. It would be easy for her to give up. Although,' she said thoughtfully, 'the fact that she won't admit to the pregnancy is probably working in her favour to some extent. Hopefully, by the time she's willing to think about her situation and make the necessary arrange-

ments, she'll be on the road to seeing a career for herself
in the future.'

'I don't suppose she's ever mentioned the boy's name
to you?' He paused between mouthfuls to look at her, and
she shook her head in response.

'Not a word. Although I haven't asked, to be honest. I
did, initially, when she first told me about the situation,
but it was no use. I could see that I wouldn't get anywhere
going down that road, and I think it's something we just
can't force out of her.'

'If I ever got my hands on him…'

Rebecca eyed him sceptically. 'Just the sort of reaction
to encourage confidences.' She lowered her eyes and carried on with her salad. Funny how exhausting eating lettuce was on the mouth. She felt as though she'd been
chewing for hours and getting nowhere.

'Point taken,' he agreed reluctantly, sitting back and
closing his knife and fork. 'So we go across to France, she
practises her French, does a routine of work during the day
and…'

'You two get to know one another,' Rebecca said, filling
in the blanks. She finally gave up on the lettuce and looked
at him curiously.

'So tell me, what *does* one chat to a teenage girl about?'
He tried to distract her attention from the seriousness of
the question by making a big deal out of calling the wine
waiter across and ordering a carafe of wine, but he had
flushed darkly.

So *that* was the reason for this little lunchtime rendez-
vous, she thought. He was nervous as hell about being in
the same place as Emily, and he wanted to pick her brain
for hints on how he could get through the optimistic month
he had set himself.

'You could try finding out about her life with her mother

in Australia,' Rebecca suggested mildly. 'That's a pretty big subject.'

The shutters clamped down over his eyes. God, was he like his daughter, if only he could see it.

'I have no intention of discussing any such thing.'

'Why not?'

'Why not?' He looked at her as though amazed that she should have the temerity to ask the question in the first place, never mind wait for an answer. She looked back at him blandly. 'You're encroaching on private territory,' he informed her coldly.

'Which is something you're fond of doing yourself.'

'I'm not one of your students. I guess you teachers end up feeling as though you have a right to other people's thoughts, whatever they may be, but you're way out of line here, lady.'

Rebecca shrugged. 'Fine by me. I don't care one way or the other myself what you think of your ex-wife. You asked me what you could find to talk about with your daughter. I went for the most obvious topic.' What *did* he think of his ex-wife, she wondered, and why? They must have parted company on pretty hostile terms and she could feel sheer curiosity biting away at her.

'Good. Just as long as you understand where my boundaries lie.' He gave her a quick glance and this time it was her turn to raise her eyebrows in amusement. 'Care to share the joke?' he asked aggressively. 'You think it's humorous that I've reminded you what you're here to do? Sort out my daughter?'

'Did I look as though I was enjoying a joke?' she asked innocently, absent-mindedly watching the waiter as he disappeared with their starters. 'Please accept my apologies,' she said, returning her attention to Nicholas who was now scowling. 'So, as topics go, your daughter's past is off limits, Hmm.'

'And you can wipe that look off your face,' he muttered. 'Veronica was a bitch who got pregnant on purpose because she wanted all the trappings I could offer her. We were like chalk and cheese and as soon as she discovered that she made a point of making my life a living hell, but I was willing to stick it out for the sake of the baby. That, unfortunately, was not good enough. She made it quite clear what her terms were. We were an ill-matched couple and if we stayed together, she informed me in no uncertain terms, fidelity would not be playing a part in the arrangement. What she hadn't banked on was that I wouldn't co-operate with the game.'

He twirled the stem of his wineglass and then downed the contents in two gulps. 'I think it enraged her that I hadn't the time or patience for her and two years after Emily was born she went to Australia and her relatives over there.' His glass was refilled, but he didn't drink. Instead he stared broodingly at it, playing with the glass stem.

'I tried for custody, but I didn't have a hope in hell of getting it. For a start, she was already out of the country, and I was effectively unable to look after a young baby. Every letter and present was apparently destroyed and she threatened to scream assault if I tried following her to Australia.' He finally looked at her. 'There. Satisfied? You managed to drag my past out of me. Now do you wonder why I don't want to have too many lengthy, bonding conversations with Emily on the subject?'

'I didn't *ask* for any explanations from you…'

'No, you just managed to force them out of me. Where the hell is the food? I have a meeting this afternoon.' He looked around him impatiently.

'We could always scrap the rest of the meal.'

'Stop being so damned obliging!'

'Okay.'

'So what about *you*?' he threw at her. 'Many lovers over the years?'

'What?'

'You heard me. How many men have you taken to bed with you over the years?'

'That's none of your business!'

'You overstepped my line; now it's my turn.'

With weak relief she spotted their waiter heading towards them, plates in hand. Saved by the salmon. In an effort to deter him, she took her time choosing her vegetables, then launched into lengthy praise about the presentation of the food, which seemed to throw the waiter into a state of nervous tension. Eventually he edged away, by which time she had gathered herself together.

'I should steer clear of trying to prise information out of her about the pregnancy,' she said, neatly deflecting the conversation away from herself—something which was not lost on Nicholas.

'How many men?'

'You could ask her about her schoolwork. She's quite a genius at maths and, as if that's not enough, she's creative.'

'Were they good?'

'As a very last resort, there's always clothes.' She buried herself in her food and steadfastly ignored his interruptions although she could feel her neck burning. 'Although I don't suppose you'd have much to say on the subject.'

'Did you miss me after you'd walked out?'

'Then there are her hobbies. Ask her what she enjoys doing with her spare time and try not to remind her that spare time is something she won't have much of in a few months' time.' She didn't dare look at him. She didn't want to risk looking at those dark, intent eyes. Better to stare at her diminishing plate of salmon.

'Why won't you answer me?' he asked softly, and her eyes flickered to his face.

'Because…because it's none of your business.' Why was he tormenting her? How was it that he could unravel the cool, controlled exterior that had become the official stamp of being a teacher?

'Okay,' he acquiesced, but something in his smile made a mockery of his sudden surrender. Her apprehension at this one-month so-called holiday went up another few notches. If this carried on, she would have to be dragged to the plane kicking and screaming from under the bed.

'Enjoying the food?' he asked solicitously, and she nodded and mumbled something. 'Good. A bit different from school food, I should think.' Upon which he obligingly launched into an amusing monologue on the school food that was served up to him when he was at boarding-school, leaving her time to get her tattered nerves back into some sort of shape.

She was still resoundingly glad when they had finished eating, however, and when the dessert menu was brought round she politely refused and reminded him about the meeting he had mentioned earlier.

'Good heavens! I'd completely forgotten. The company was so riveting.'

'Sarcasm is the lowest form of humour,' she said haughtily, a little deflated when he laughed softly.

'Was I being sarcastic? I had no idea.' But at least he got the bill, and it was only as she stuck her feet back into her shoes that she was reminded of how sore they were. She could feel the holes at her heels where the skin had ruptured the fine nylon and as she stood up she grimaced as the blisters pushed against the backs of the shoes. Let this be a lesson to her, she thought silently. Large feet were not destined for long walks in delicate shoes. She had planned on taking the Underground back to the house and only catching a taxi at the other end, but the prospect of even that short walk from the restaurant to the tube station was enough to make her wince. Were a few items of clothing worth a lifetime in crutches? she wondered.

'You're hobbling.'

'What?'

They were halfway across the restaurant and she had been eyeing the exit with a certain amount of desperation. She hadn't noticed him staring at her as she walked next to him.

'You're hobbling. Why?'

'My feet are hurting,' she told him. 'I'm not accustomed to walking long distances in these shoes. I thought that they'd be all right. They've never been uncomfortable before, but then again I've never walked half of London in them before either.'

'Silly girl,' he murmured under his breath, taking her by her elbow. She felt a sharp rush of heat race through her although she kept her face steadfastly averted. In an attempt not to lean against him, she swung the opposite way and gritted her teeth together as she strode upright towards the door and eased herself into her coat.

'Now we'll take you home, make sure you get back in one piece.'

'*Take me home? Make sure I get back in one piece?*' Her voice was shrill. 'I'll be fine! A few blisters is hardly a matter of life and death!'

He wasn't listening to her. He was busy hailing a taxi, which slid over to them, leaving her just enough time to say, 'Your meeting! What about your meeting?' She was not setting foot inside the taxi until she was sure that he wouldn't be climbing in beside her. She'd had enough of her self-control being scrambled for one day.

'Ted can manage without me,' he said smoothly, out-staring her until she was forced to slide into the seat reluctantly and watch with dismay as he got in behind her and slammed the door.

'This really isn't necessary,' she began. 'I'm fully capable of taking care of myself.' He was sitting very close to her. She could feel the pressure of his arm against hers.

'No trouble at all,' he said breezily. 'Good practice. I mean, I'm going to have to get accustomed to delegating some of my workload when we go to France, wouldn't you agree?' He loosened his tie. 'Very odd, looking at the world through a taxi window and not being in a hurry to get somewhere fast. Good Lord, the streets are crowded. What are all these people doing here at this time of day?'

'Relaxing,' Rebecca offered wryly, wishing she could count herself in their number but her stress levels were rising rapidly.

'They certainly don't seem to be in too much of a hurry,' he agreed, staring out of the window on her side.

The car only picked up a bit of speed once they were out of the busy streets and heading back towards the house, which was ominously silent when they arrived. No sign of Emily, and Rebecca sighed to herself. Where was the child? Had she done her work? What on earth could she possibly have found to do on a weekday, when all her friends would have been at school?

She would sort that out later. Her priority was to get rid of Nicholas as speedily as she could. She felt a bit treacherous, considering it was *his* house, but in the circumstances she could live with the feeling.

She walked as confidently as she could towards the sitting room, sat down and kicked off her shoes. It was the first time she had examined her feet and her exclamation of horror was drowned by his. He was kneeling on the ground in front of her and she felt her body freeze as he gently took one of her feet in his big hands and examined the raw patches caused by the shoes.

'My God, woman. You must have been in agony! We'll have to get these seen to. Take off your stockings.'

'Tights,' Rebecca said in confusion. 'I don't wear stockings, and I can patch them up myself.' Her voice reeked with mortification and she wanted to yank her foot out of his hand, but he was holding her firmly, too firmly for her to take that course of action.

'I'll go get some stuff to bathe them. Tights off by the time I return.'

It was no use. Either she remained where she was and found herself removing her tights in his presence or else she obeyed and let him get on with it. She whipped them off in seconds and sat back down, her heart beating fast. Whilst he was out of the room, she took the opportunity to primly arrange her skirt around her, covering the maximum of exposed flesh.

He returned with a basin of warm water, various tubes and a packet of plasters.

'Really,' she tried again, weakly, 'there's no need...'

'Keep quiet, woman.' He squatted down and she stared at his dark head, wanting to divorce herself from the sensations generated by the feel of his hands on her foot. He worked slowly and with surprising gentleness for someone as large as he was. It felt delicious. She allowed herself to lean back against the sofa and close her eyes. The cream, whatever it was, was soothing and it was only when he had finished and she realised that he was gently massaging her foot that her eyes sprang back open and she found him looking at her with a curious smile on his face.

'Wh-what are you doing?' she stuttered, wriggling her foot to get free.

'Getting your blood circulation going,' he said soothingly.

'There's nothing wrong with my blood circulation!'

'Who can tell?' he mused. 'Those were some pretty bad blisters. There's no telling what it's done to your blood circulation.' He was still playing with her foot, which was the most luxurious feeling in the world.

They were absorbed like this, Rebecca racking her brains to say something and knowing that she should repossess her foot which was feeling altogether too comfortable in his hands for her liking, when the door was pushed open and Emily stood there, framed in a pose of frozen surprise.

They both looked at her and in a split second, as Rebecca realised what sort of little tableau they were presenting, she pulled her foot out of his hands.

'I didn't think that you were in,' she said, cursing herself for saying just the wrong thing completely. 'Have you done that work I set for you?'

'All done, teacher, dear.' She strolled in and circled them with barely concealed enjoyment.

'I hope I haven't interrupted anything?' Her mouth was trembling now with laughter and she let the question hang in the air.

Nicholas stood up, taking his time. 'Of course you haven't,' he said dryly. 'If we had been doing anything worth interrupting, don't you think we would have had the foresight to lock the door?'

Which brought a violent rush of colour to his daughter's face and instantly wiped the smirk off. He was grinning now, highly amused by her sudden discomfort. Rebecca just wanted to sink deep into the chair and disappear altogether.

'Take care of those feet of yours,' he said sternly, turning to her. 'Hope one of your purchases was some slightly more comfortable shoes.' He gave her one of those transforming smiles of his and this time there was an implied sharing of a joke. She reluctantly grinned back and grinned even more when she saw Emily narrow her eyes in suspicion.

'So what was *that* all about?' she asked, throwing herself on to a chair as soon as her father had left the room.

'Go and bring me that work I set for you. We might just as well go through it now.'

'Not till you've answered my question,' she persisted, pouting.

Rebecca sighed. 'It's not what you think so you'd better not let your imagination go roaming. I met your father for lunch…'

'You met my father for lunch?' she squealed gleefully.

'To discuss *you.*'

'Oh.'

'And I was stupid enough to go shopping beforehand in these ridiculous shoes—' she kicked one lightly '—and my feet erupted with blisters.'

'So?'

'So your father kindly offered to bring me home and sort them out. Actually, he insisted.' She did not feel like a teacher during this explanation. She felt like a teenager confessing to inappropriate behaviour.

'He *insisted* on bringing you back here so that he could play with your feet?' She looked up in the air and snorted with disbelief. 'That does *not* sound a bit like my father.'

'Which is why you've probably read him all wrong,' Rebecca said quickly, crossing her fingers behind her back.

'Smells fishy to me. First he breaks up with the odious Fiona, then he's caught rubbing your feet...sure there's nothing you want to tell me about?'

Rebecca flung a cushion in her general direction, which Emily dodged, before springing up and tossing her hair back. 'Well, I'll go fetch my work and just to put your mind at ease...' she sauntered towards the door '...I can think of *lots* of women I'd like less in the role of step-mother!'

Rebecca could still hear her laughter as she headed out of the room, amused at finding her teacher in a clinch, even if it was innocent.

Stepmother? No. It would not do for Emily to start get-ting any ideas in that direction at all. It had been folly to allow Nicholas to tend to her wretched blisters, which she could easily have done herself, and it had been even greater folly to assume that Emily was out of the house. Everything had been innocent, she argued to herself, but in the eyes of an imaginative and unpredictable teenager certain interpretations could be put on the scene that had confronted her, and Lord only knew how far they would stoke Emily's feverish mind.

She groaned to herself, and even though Emily did not openly raise the subject for the remainder of the day there were enough oblique looks and secret smiles to confirm the worst.

She waited in the sitting room until after eleven, long after Emily had retired for the night, and confronted Nicholas as he walked through the door.

'We need to have a chat,' were her opening words. If he was a little startled to be confronted by her at such an odd hour, he hid it well.

'Fond of these little surprise chats, aren't you?' he said, divesting himself of his jacket and tie and slinging them both over the banister. 'I guess it's pointless asking whether it could wait?' He raked his fingers through his hair and gave her a long, unreadable look, then he sighed and nodded in the direction of the kitchen. 'I suppose I could do with a cup of coffee. It's been a hell of a day.' He began walking towards the kitchen, and Rebecca followed in his wake.

'Has it? Why?'

He began filling the kettle, and without even being conscious of it she absorbed every detail of his movements, the lines of his body, the way his trousers hung slightly down his waist so that his muscular, lean-hipped build was unmistakable. The width of his shoulders gave him an aggressively powerful look and underneath the white of his work shirt she could see the ripple of muscle. 'Because there's a heck of a lot to do before we leave. I've been in a series of meetings all day, and believe me when I tell you that they're damn tiring.'

'Oh, I do believe you,' Rebecca said sympathetically. 'I attend a few myself. They always overrun and I'm always exhausted at the end of them.'

He propped himself against the kitchen counter and looked at her speculatively. 'Yes, I suppose you do. Tell me, do you miss it?'

'Miss what?'

'Being in a school environment as opposed to private home tuition.'

'I've not been here long enough to reach an opinion on that,' Rebecca hedged, uncomfortably aware of his eyes on her. He had amazing eyes. This was yet one more detail she found herself absorbing. They were so dark that it was impossible to read anything from them. 'It's different from working at a school.' She shrugged awkwardly. 'I guess I feel as though it's a kind of break from my normal routine.'

'Well, tell me if you start feeling differently.'

'And you'll do what?'

'Persuade you to stay.' He poured some milk straight from the bottle into his mug and held it to his lips, looking at her over the rim. 'Well, you didn't expect me to say, Let you go, did you? Not after I had to drag you here in the first place kicking and screaming.'

'That's not fair or true.'

'Anyway, what did you want to chat to me about?' he said, sidestepping her. 'Not another rethink on this holiday, I hope. My secretary has sorted out something in France and she won't take too kindly to unravelling the lot and starting over. She hasn't earned her nickname, Dragon Dee, for nothing. In fact, she reminds me a lot of our treasure Mrs Dunne.'

'Your secretary is…?'

'Celebrating her sixtieth birthday in two weeks' time, has the disposition of a thwarted tyrant and the femininity of a rhinoceros.' He grinned fondly at the thought of it.

'Then why do you…?' She was genuinely bewildered. She would have thought that Nicholas Knight, the man who liked his women to look like Christmas tree ornaments, would have had a secretary who fitted the mould, who was visually appealing and fussed over him with girlish admiration.

'Because she's damned good at her job.' He gulped back a mouthful of coffee and continued to look at her. 'And because, despite what that feverish little mind of yours is thinking, the last thing I need is a chit of a girl who looks at me with longing eyes whenever I ask her to type something and gets into a tizzy if she's done something wrong.'

He gave her a slow, leisurely smile. 'We all learn from experience, don't we? I've had a couple of those and their careers with me were as short as their skirts. I much prefer longing looks to be directed at me outside the work environment.' His smile now was more wicked and leisurely. 'In case you'd like to take note.'

Rebecca's mouth snapped shut and she folded her arms in a businesslike manner.

'Actually,' she said crisply, looking past his amused, sexy face to the bottle-green tiled wall just behind him, 'you've brought me neatly round to what I wanted to say. That little scene that Emily walked in on earlier today— that *perfectly innocent* little scene—has let loose her imagination. She's been dropping hints all day about love and romance and giving me sidelong, knowing looks. I just thought that I'd mention it to you because I know you'll agree with me that it's not a good idea that she gets any mistaken impressions about our relationship. Lord knows what pregnancy has done to her state of mind. Anyway, I felt I had to warn you so that we…we…'

'Keep our passion a bit more firmly under wraps?'

'It's not funny!'

'Yes, it is, and why are you so hot under the collar about the whole thing if it was all so innocent?'

'Stop being deliberately difficult!' She finally looked at him and realised that he was laughing softly to himself, which made her feel even more flustered than she already did.

'I'm sorry.'

'No, you're not! Emily is young and impressionable. I don't want her to be left with the wrong ideas.' She'd said her piece and she walked towards the door, head held high, arms still folded, making sure that she didn't get too close to him.

'In that case,' he called airily after her departing figure, 'you'll have to make sure not to tempt me into any tricky situations, won't you?'

She stopped and glared at him. 'Nothing could be further from my mind!'

'Oh, good! What a relief!' He was still grinning with enjoyment. 'Because I can't help but cast my mind back to when you were young and naïve and…' He let the words hang unfinished in the air, allowing her imagination to neatly fill in the blanks.

She stared at him, unable to come up with any smart response. Her head was a jumble of incoherent thoughts, none of them too flattering.

'Was that all?' he asked, when the silence threatened to become deafening. 'Because I'm dog-tired and bed beckons…'

Bed! She pictured him sprawled in masculine abandon on his king-sized bed, and fled.

CHAPTER SEVEN

EMILY grumbled for the entire journey. From the minute they left the house by taxi for Gatwick airport to the minute they touched down at the Nantes Atlantique airport.

It was a lousy time to go anywhere on holiday, and if they had to go, why did it have to be France? She wasn't sure whether she'd packed enough clothes or too many— not that it mattered because she hated them all anyway. What was she going to do with her spare time? Did they seriously expect her to sit with her father and chat? Whose brilliant idea had it been anyway?

Rebecca spent most of the flight across gazing out of the window and attempting to read her guidebook, which was difficult when every other paragraph was punctuated by yet another complaint, or else a rehash of a previous one.

The only bright spot on the horizon was the fact that Nicholas would be joining them the following day because he had been held up in Frankfurt in a meeting that had failed to run according to schedule.

'It's going to be so *unbearably dull*,' Emily brooded as they climbed into a taxi outside the airport and waited while the driver stacked their suitcases into the boot. 'And *cold*.'

'Shall I tell you all about the Loire Valley?' Rebecca asked, immune to the litany of complaints that had been buzzing around her ears for the past two and a half hours.

'I can't think of anything I'd less like to hear about.' Emily stared out of the window with a sulky expression as the taxi moved away from the airport and began heading towards their destination.

With typical style, Nicholas had managed to arrange one month in the Loire Valley, staying in an original stone farmhouse that belonged to a family friend who only used the place intermittently.

'There'll be things to do, but not too many distractions, and it's very peaceful there. Just the sort of place for Emily to do some hard thinking about her life,' he'd said.

It had sounded ideal. Even now, coping with Emily's lack of enthusiasm had not been enough to daunt the little flame of excitement that had begun to burn inside Rebecca. The downside would be Nicholas, but then the upside would be some remarkable French countryside, glorious châteaux and churches and, of course, the vineyards.

'I hope this place isn't run-down and shabby,' Emily contributed, half an hour after they had left the airport.

'Why do you think it might be?'

She shrugged and rested against the back of the seat. 'Well, you never know,' was all she could suggest in an ominous voice. 'It's a *stone* farmhouse, of all things. Everyone knows that stone places have no central heating. We'll probably freeze to death there, all in a stab at family bonding.'

'You're such an irresistible optimist,' Rebecca said, laughing. 'And I guess if we don't freeze to death we'll get lost walking somewhere in the countryside, or else we'll be savaged by a couple of stray cows.'

'Oh, very amusing,' Emily said, smiling reluctantly.

But the complaints grew less repetitive as they drove towards Berry. The countryside was absorbing. A rolling landscape, punctuated with the graceful spectacle of vineyards. Ever so often, they would pass a sign offering *dégustations* or wine tastings. Concealed in the remarkable landscape, Rebecca imagined the châteaux, elegantly dominating the hills and fields.

It was a far cry from London.

She was still engrossed in the scenery when they finally reached the small village where they would be staying, a few kilometres from Bourges.

The taxi driver, who had abandoned his attempts at conversation early on, in the face of Emily's unresponsiveness, now came alive with his description of the châteaux and abbeys they could explore. He had grown up not far from where they would be staying, he explained, and was suffused with pride at the beauty of his native region.

Emily yawned as Rebecca conversed with the man in French, keeping her vocabulary as simple as she could rather than become immersed in linguistic difficulties. Her French was passable but rusty.

'*Et voilà!*' he exclaimed, gesturing to a grey- and sepia-coloured building which they had approached via a network of charming country lanes.

'We're here!' Rebecca said breathlessly. 'Isn't it beautiful, Emily? Now don't be such a dog in the manger. Admit it. It's absolutely gorgeous!'

The roof was broad and very low, with four windows peeping out and a chimney cutting it in half and stretching towards the ground. On one side, towards the front, was a small, rather exquisite miniature turret and at the back a much larger mill-like edifice which afforded the place the look of something unique and slightly eccentric.

And behind the farmhouse was a dense bank of trees and bushes. Some of the trees were close enough to sprawl languidly against the sides of the mill at the back so that they appeared to be on the brink of taking over completely.

'It's all right, I suppose,' Emily said, unwilling to commit herself to admiring something she had made up her mind to dislike on sight.

'And the village is only a fifteen-minute walk away,' Rebecca carried on. 'We could stroll down there a bit later. What do you say? Game?'

'Humph.'

'What an unpleasant little creature you are,' Rebecca teased, fishing the house key out of her bag and inserting it into the lock. She had come to the conclusion that reprimanding Emily for her moodiness or insinuating that she should be grateful for what she had were not necessarily the right approaches to adopt. She tended to launch into heated debates on the subject, whereas a bit of gentle teasing was something that disarmed her.

Nicholas had given her keys to the house and told her that there would be some basic food provided by the housekeeper who looked after the place twice a week, winter and summer, whether it was occupied or not.

'At least it's not *too* cold here,' Emily was saying grudgingly. 'Not as cold as it was in London when we left.'

'So you reckon the freezing-to-death scenario is no longer in the cards...'

She pushed open the front door and they walked in. Even Emily gasped. The house was old, but had been tastefully modernised and impeccably decorated. Huge, ornate tapestries dominated the walls and instead of a cold stone floor there was thick cream carpeting that made Rebecca want to kick off her shoes and sink her toes in.

It was by no means a large farmhouse, but it was sumptuous. They had walked directly into the sitting area, which lay at one side of the front door and was positioned around a large, open fireplace, complete with logs ready for use. Towards the opposite side of the house she could glimpse through the doorway the kitchen. In the middle of the room a sturdy staircase led upwards, presumably to the bed-rooms, and as her eyes travelled up she could see that they had been designed around a galleried balcony which over-looked the sitting room.

The driver, who appeared to be as taken with the place as they were, reluctantly accepted his fare and generous tip and cast a few backward glances before he closed the front door behind him.

'There's a telly,' Emily said, dumping her hand luggage on the ground and looking around her.

'Nothing like getting your priorities right, is there?' Rebecca said dryly. 'Come on, groucho, let's explore.'

It was bigger than she had first thought. There were five bedrooms in the main area of the farmhouse, with two bathrooms, and the mill attached to the back had been converted into a small den with a small sitting area un-derneath, both linked by a winding iron staircase.

Somewhere for Nicholas to work. She found it hard to believe that he would go anywhere without having access of some sort to his various companies.

When he arrived later that night, she would encourage him into a routine that involved him being stuck up in the den, at least for part of the day, while she and Emily did their work and explored the village.

As it turned out, he needed very little encouragement.

Rebecca, sitting in the café opposite Emily, thoughtfully sipped from her over-sized cup of coffee and acknowl-edged, with some surprise, that the past week had gone very smoothly indeed.

Nicholas had arrived in a rented car, and so far had been on his best behaviour. In the mornings, they all trooped down to the same little café in the centre of the village and had a breakfast of croissants and coffee, and Nicholas invariably took the opportunity to scour the French newspapers. He would chat intermittently, but with his attention half distracted by whatever he was reading Emily did not feel threatened or uncomfortable, so that the little start to each day was at least lacking in rancour.

Then he would take himself back to the farmhouse where he worked solidly until lunchtime, and the remainder of the day was spent with them.

She couldn't believe how easygoing he had been. There had been no confrontations with his daughter, even though there had likewise been no spectacular bonding. They both tended to use Rebecca as a mediator and she had become adept at heading off potentially sticky situations. She was getting quite accustomed to exclaiming brightly, 'What a beautiful piece of architecture! I'll just read a bit about this from my guidebook, shall I?'

Or, 'Shall we try and speak only in French for the duration of this meal?' Which was always effective because arguments were almost impossible in a foreign language.

In the evenings, Emily would do her disappearing act until food was on the table, then she would emerge and eat in virtual silence, responding to her father's attempts at conversation with casual, polite indifference. But at least she had not been showing her teeth. At least her routine of storming out and slamming doors had gone into hibernation.

'Is it okay if I go for a stroll in the village by myself?'

Rebecca snapped out of her thoughts and looked at Emily, who was looking particularly attractive in a pair of jeans, a thick cream jumper and a cream trench coat that reached to mid-thigh. Her cheeks were pink and she had tied her hair into a ponytail which took years off her face. She looked like a charming, pretty schoolgirl.

'By yourself?'

'Yes, by myself. I don't need you and Dad chaperoning me every hour of the day! What do you think I'm going to get up to?'

'Well, your track record hasn't proved too reliable, has it?' Rebecca responded tartly, and the girl flushed and looked away.

Amazingly, she had still made no mention of the pregnancy, even though Rebecca had tried to corner her on the subject a couple of times.

'It's boring sitting here drinking coffee while you read your guidebook,' she said sulkily, playing with her mug. 'And you can't say that I haven't been doing all that work you brought over.'

'Well...' Rebecca hesitated '...you can have a wander for an hour, then we'll meet back here.' Having explored various châteaux, abbeys and of course the delights of Bourges, they had decided to spend the afternoon relaxing in the local village.

'Great.' She sprang to her feet with the alacrity of someone who knew they should seize the chance and was out of the door before Rebecca could add any more provisions to the clause.

She was staring blankly out of the window and debating whether she should indulge in a calorie-ridden mid-afternoon treat, when she saw Nicholas crossing the road. He was the last person she had expected to see. He had informed them that they had the afternoon to themselves because he would be involved in an unavoidable conference call.

'Buy lots of fruit!' he had instructed Rebecca as they'd set off for the village on foot. 'It's what a growing girl needs.' Whereupon he'd shot his daughter a meaningful look.

So what was he doing here now? It was such a surprise

that Rebecca found herself blinking hard to clear her head of the illusion.

No illusion. He was very real and all the more alarming because she had become accustomed to having Emily around as her own chaperon. There had been very few instances when they had been alone together and certainly none of them had lasted long enough for any kind of conversation to develop.

He had seen her. It wouldn't have been difficult. She loved this particular coffee shop and he knew that. Even when she was in one of her self-sacrificing frames of mind, she still adored drooling over all the pastries that reclined temptingly behind glass.

He swept into the shop now and headed straight for her table, only pausing in passing to order them each a crumbly tart of enormous proportions and oozing with fresh custard.

'What are you doing here?' Rebecca asked. 'I thought you had a conference call to make.'

'No need to sound so disappointed,' Nicholas said wryly. 'The conference call's been postponed until the end of the week. Apparently a virulent stomach bug has wiped out fifty per cent of our German contributors, so I thought I'd take a stroll down here and see what you two were up to.'

'I'm up to finishing my coffee, and Emily's gone for a little walk in the town. She's rebelling against being chaperoned everywhere she goes, and I do admit that she has a point. She's not a child and if she wants a bit of free time now and again, then maybe it's not such a bad idea. Good chance for her to use her French, anyway. I hope you don't mind?'

He pushed one of the pastries towards her before answering and she looked at it with suspicion, as though afraid that if she didn't pick it up it might just leap off the plate into her salivating mouth anyway.

'It's bad for my figure.'

Not such a good thing to say, because he took that as an opportunity to assess her with leisurely thoroughness. She had been lulled into a false sense of security ever since they had come to France. There had been no personal conversations, none of that wicked charm that he had used on her intermittently in the past. He had been a good boy.

'You have a striking figure,' he murmured. 'I can't see that indulging in one pastry is going to change that.'

'Girls with large frames need to watch what they eat,' Rebecca said starchily.

'You *have* got a large frame, haven't you?' he commented, with enough appreciation in his voice to turn a potential insult into something alarmingly different. 'It was one of the first things that attracted me to you.'

Rebecca could feel herself squirming. If her hair could have blushed, it would have.

'I like being appreciated for my mind, actually,' she mumbled, and he nodded gravely.

'Oh, yes, your mind fires on all fronts as well.'

She had to. How could she be expected to handle Nicholas Knight in a playful mood without sustenance? She gave in to the pastry.

'So,' he said with a rapid change of voice. 'How do you think this holiday is working out so far?'

'Pretty good, actually.' Dignity and pastry consumption were two things that didn't go hand in hand. She tried to eat delicately, but she was aware of the inelegant picture she presented. Crumbs everywhere, one hand holding the pastry, the other attempting to forestall any wayward blobs of custard. She finished her mouthful and sat back, flicking her jeans to clear the crumbs. 'She's certainly been less emotional over here than she was in England, she's been doing all the work set and without a great deal of effort, and her French is coming on a treat.'

'She still dodges my company, though, doesn't she?'

'Not to the same extent, surely.'

'No,' he admitted, not managing to conceal his pleasure. 'At least she's stopped treating me routinely as the enemy. Now all we have to do is engineer a discussion of the pregnancy.'

'Easier said than done,' Rebecca told him. 'If there were *some* outward signs of it, then she might actually take in the fact that it's *happening*, but so far she's been one of those lucky people who have no morning sickness, no lethargy and her mood swings are so normal anyway that it's hard to tell whether they're hormone-induced or not.' She was about to expand on the subject when Emily strolled through the door towards them, her face beaming. Absolutely radiant.

'Where have *you* materialised from?' she asked her father, though her voice was so cheery that the sting of the words, for once, was lost.

'Funny. This has a feeling of *déjà vu* about it,' he answered, shifting his chair slightly to accommodate Emily's. 'A stomach bug has wiped out most of my conference-call participants, so I wandered down here. You're in a good mood.'

They were speaking to one another! And there was no underlying tension! Rebecca held her breath, waiting for the spell to break.

'Just enjoying the freedom of being away from you two.'

'Oh, thank you very much!' Rebecca interjected in a mock-hurt voice, and Emily threw her a sheepish smile.

'You know what I mean.' She picked up a few crumbs

from her father's plate with the pads of her finger and licked them away. 'It's a nice little place and it's great to look around without one or both of you breathing over my shoulder.' She glanced across to Nicholas from under her lashes. 'I don't suppose I could have the rest of the afternoon free to stroll around, could I? I've discovered some great little shops tucked away down a side road. Antique clothes and stuff.'

'Antique clothes?' Nicholas's brow creased in puzzlement. 'What *are* antique clothes, exactly?'

'Lots of embroidery—you know.'

'Embroidery?' he asked, surprised. Emily was not an embroidery kind of girl. Black Lycra and thick tights, yes. But embroidery?

'Well, it makes a change,' Emily muttered, heading towards an argument but stopping short in time. 'I promise to be back home in under two hours. I'd just go back there and have another look and perhaps sit and watch the world go by.' She dropped her eyes and, like a musician striking just the right chord, said in a forlorn voice, 'It would do my French no end of good and...' she twiddled the small stem of the rose vase in the centre of the table '...it would give me time to think...'

Rebecca caught Nicholas's eye and he gave her a slight nod.

'Well,' she said, still hesitating for reasons she wasn't quite sure of, 'if you promise to be home no later than...' she looked at her watch '...five o'clock.'

'Great!' She stood up, apparently now bored with their company, and disappeared out of the door.

'Might do her some good,' Nicholas said thoughtfully. 'Perhaps she needs a little space to sort herself out, and the weather is great for browsing round shops. Crisp and clear. Might rub off on that brain of hers.'

'There's nothing wrong with your daughter's brain,' Rebecca smiled. 'If anything, it's a little too active for her own good.'

'What harm can it do?' he pointed out logically. 'It's not as though she's going to get into trouble. She's already reached that particular place.'

The idea of the pregnancy was one that he had slowly become accustomed to. After the initial shock, he had come to terms with it, although he had never said as much to her.

They walked back to the house, Nicholas holding the bags of groceries she had bought as though they weighed less than nothing, and on the way made impersonal chat. It was only as they neared the front door that she realised with nervous alarm that they would now have two hours closeted together without Emily as a convenient third party.

What was she so scared of? She couldn't put her finger on it. So he had flirted with her now and again. That meant nothing because he was a man to whom flirting was second nature. He would probably flirt quite merrily with someone's great-grandmother. So they had known each other once, briefly. It was history. She was a completely different person now, and so was he. It wasn't even as if they had had a long-standing, meaningful relationship.

So why did the thought of spending time alone in his company send her into a state of suppressed panic?

It was ridiculous.

'I'll go and prepare tonight's dinner,' she said quickly, as soon as they had stepped through the front door and divested themselves of their overcoats. She had clutched the bag of groceries in one hand and was virtually backing towards the kitchen door!

'I'll give you a hand.'

'No need!' she squeaked. 'Feel free to carry on with your work! I wouldn't want to disrupt your routine!'

'The most enjoyable part of any routine is disrupting it.' He gave a crooked smile and walked towards her, his hands in his pockets. 'I don't know about you, but that always makes me feel like a kid again, playing truant.'

'You played truant?' Rebecca asked in a high-pitched voice. Her feet felt as though they had been welded to the ground, and only a huge effort of will enabled her to un-pluck them and spin around towards the kitchen before he descended on her completely.

'Don't we all at some point in our lives? I didn't make a habit of it, but I have to admit on the few occasions I did it my adrenaline hit the roof.' She heard him laugh softly behind her at the memory of it.

'I never did.' She deposited the food on the table and began reaching for chopping boards and knives and bowls and anything that could distract her from his presence. She had planned on making a quiche, one of her specialities, albeit with the aid of pre-packed pastry, and she now whipped her vegetables out of the carrier bag, still not looking at him, and began washing them under the tap. Presumably he had located himself on a chair by the table and would hopefully grow bored being a spectator to a mediocre cook, and take himself off.

'Never?'

'No. Are you sure you want to stay here? I hate having people loom over me when I'm preparing food.'

'Loom?' With her back to him as she stood at the sink, she could still hear the amused chuckle in his voice. 'This is looming.' Her head was so full of confused thoughts that she didn't even hear him approaching until he was standing close to her, leaning over her, breathing against her cheek. She jumped back and hit his hard body.

'Don't be so anxious,' he said soothingly. 'I just came over to get myself a glass of water.' He leaned past her and filled a glass and then resumed his position three inches away from her. She could feel her heart beating wildly. One small step closer and her breasts would touch his chest. Desperately, she stared at his neck, onion in one hand and knife in the other.

'Anxious? Anxious? Who's anxious?' Her intention had been to laugh in a dismissive way, but she ended up sounding faintly maniacal instead.

'You are.' He drank some of the water, rested the glass in the sink, then he gently removed the knife and the onion from her. 'I'm not a fool. Despite everything you've said, you're relaxed here because Emily's around all of the time.'

'That's crazy!'

'You make me a little jumpy as well, as a matter of fact, although that has nothing to do with nerves. When I look at you, the years travel backwards and I'm that young man again, panting and eager.'

'No.' Her legs felt wobbly. She wasn't conditioned to deal with this sort of situation. She was conditioned to handle children and teenagers, to impose control on them, just as she had unconsciously ended up imposing control on all her boyfriends in the past. She just wasn't conditioned to deal with emotions that were all over the place and a man who turned all her self-control to jelly.

'No, what? No, I wasn't panting and eager all those years ago? I was, you know. I liked that air of innocence you carried around with you. It excited me then and it excites me now.'

'I've grown up,' Rebecca whispered helplessly, wanting to block her ears in a childish reaction of denial. 'I don't have an air of innocence around me now! Maybe when I was younger, but I'm a teacher!'

'So you are,' he agreed easily, 'and you cling to that every time you feel the ground slipping away from under your feet. Do you think I haven't noticed you looking at me out of the corner of your eye? Hot little looks when you think I'm not aware? When you think I'm involved in inspecting some stained-glass window or ornate ceiling?'

She hadn't even been aware that she had been doing that! But now she realised that he was right. She stole looks at him and filed them away in her memory banks and replayed them late at night when no one was around. And he had noticed. She blushed with mortification to think that he had noticed, that she had been so transparent.

'That's not true,' she protested weakly.

'Yes, it is.' His low, mesmerising voice made a mockery of her feeble denial. 'It's nothing to be ashamed of. Being attracted to someone isn't a crime against humanity. Anyway, I like it. I steal quite a few looks at you myself, when I know your attention's somewhere else.' His hands had somehow found their way to her upper arms without her noticing and she was aware of him stroking her through her cotton shirt.

'No. Emily is…'

'Temporarily out of the house,' he finished for her, in that velvety, sexy voice of his.

'We can't…it's unethical…' She wasn't saying the right things. She could hear the hesitancy in her voice but she seemed incapable of doing anything about it.

'Unethical for…whom? This isn't a school environment. I'm not the principal and you're not my co-worker.'

'But I work for you.'

'That doesn't bother me. Why should it bother you?'

'Because…because…' The sheer agony of wanting him

and knowing that it would be all wrong, that it would engender an impossible situation, made every nerve in her body ache.

His hands had now moved from her upper arms to the altogether more dangerous planes of her collarbone. He casually undid her top button and slipped his hands underneath to caress her.

'We're sexually attracted to one another,' he murmured huskily. 'Why be martyrs and fight it? Frustration is a very poor bed companion.'

His words, resounding in her ears, were running circles around her logical thought processes. In fact, they were completely obliterating her logical thought processes.

'So why don't we just surrender?' He touched her lips with his. Nothing urgent, nothing hungry, but that light, feathery touch was enough to make her groan weakly. 'Why don't we just give in and stop trying to pretend that it's not there?' Another light kiss, but this time she felt the brush of his tongue on her mouth. Her hands travelled, seemingly of their own volition, to his neck and her fingers slid through his hair.

Why not? her mind screamed at her. He was right. What was there to gain by denying what she felt and then having the dubious privilege of wearing a halo around her head? All the memories of how it had been between them rushed back into her head with shocking clarity.

She pulled his head down and tilted hers up, and he uttered a moan and kissed her, really kissed her, a hard, hungry kiss, ravaging her mouth with his tongue, cupping her face with his hands.

His weight pushed her back against the kitchen counter and as he continued his sensual exploration with his mouth his hands deftly undid the remainder of her buttons. He tugged apart the shirt and she could feel her chest rising and falling quickly, responding to the heat spreading through her like wildfire.

Her breasts felt heavy. She was breathing quickly, her eyes half closed, her body arched back, waiting for him to touch her breasts, her craving spiralling as he kissed her neck, then trailed his tongue along the gentle swell above the lacy edging of her bra.

She knew that her nipples were pushing against the bra, and she knew that he was enjoying knowing that they were waiting for his mouth. Feverishly, she began reaching behind her to unclasp it, but he stilled her hand, and instead scooped them out so that they fell like swollen, heavy fruits over her bra. She glanced down at his dark head and saw her own generous breasts, the nipples engorged and dark, and then leaned back to enjoy his steady, thorough suckling of them, the feel of teeth and tongue and lips rousing her to an unbearable peak of excitement.

With one hand, he worked on the button of her jeans, then pulled down the zip, and she wriggled so that he could pull them partially down; they slid to her ankles. With a few small movements, she stepped out of them. She knew, in some fuzzy part of her brain which was still operational, what he would do next, but it was an intimacy she had never before experienced, and she gasped with pleasure as he licked a path down her stomach, tugging her underwear to her feet, then flicked his tongue against the brush of soft hair.

With an instinct born of need, she parted her legs slightly and shuddered when his tongue found what it had been looking for. She felt it move rhythmically against the throbbing bud and groaned. Her whole body wanted to explode.

She couldn't recall a time when she had been aroused like this before. It was unstoppable and uncontrollable.

There was nothing civilised about what she was feeling. It was as if she was possessed by the most primitive thing in the world.

She pushed against his tongue, melting and dissolving in pools of ecstasy, soaring towards the peak of fulfilment, but before she could prematurely get there he levered himself up and undid his belt, pulling it through the loops of his trousers with a single tug. She heard it drop to the ground. As his zip was undone, she opened her eyes and was confronted by such splendid masculinity that another arrow of pleasure shot through her.

During those heady two weeks a thousand years ago, she had never actually touched him. Now she reached down and moved her hand sensuously up and down the hardened, throbbing shaft, enjoying his gasps of pleasure.

'I can't hold on much longer,' he groaned. He pulled her hand away and replaced it with his, guiding himself into the opening that waited for him, like a flower.

His first thrust was gentle enough, but then he gained momentum, pushing hard and fast until there was nothing left in her to hold back.

She came with a loud gasp and her body shivered as the wave ebbed into a multitude of little ripples, each one subsiding, giving way to another.

'Emily.'

That was her first tentative word as their bodies stilled, and he looked at her with a slow smile.

'I haven't forgotten. Shame, isn't it? Because I could do that all over again.'

So, she thought, could I.

CHAPTER EIGHT

THIS was all a dream and all dreams ended.

'What's the deep sigh for?' They were both lying naked on the bed, with the covers half strewn over them. Her head was resting on his shoulder and from her angle she could follow the smooth, hard lines of his body, down his torso to his waist, and beyond, down to his long, muscular legs. He had a beautiful body. There was no other description for it. Every time he stripped off, and the times now had been numerous, she still gave a little indrawn gasp of pleasure at his sheer physical magnificence.

At least she had lost her natural reserve at her own nudity. She had had to, because for the last two and a half weeks they had made love like sex-starved teenagers for the two hours during the day when Emily went off to the village for some 'space'.

She had nagged and insisted and cajoled, and they had given in. Rebecca was realistic enough to realise that part of the reason was that it had suited them.

And the space had done Emily a world of good. She had been in an abnormally cheerful mood for such a long time that her sulks were now passing storm clouds on a sunny horizon. And with that change of temperament relations between herself and her father had finally stuttered off to a start. They conversed, even when Rebecca was in the kitchen preparing a meal, without looking anxiously for her return as mediator.

'Hello? Where are you?' He turned his head so that their

faces were very close together and she smiled with the contentment of a well-fed cat.

'Here. But not for much longer.' She sighed again, a small, regretful sound. She had long since given up all rational thought about why they should never have begun this liaison, which was fated to go nowhere. Nothing had changed from all those years ago when she had forced herself to turn her back on a man whose life was so far removed from her own that any romantic notions of forever were delusions.

'Oh, I don't know,' he said lazily, 'we have another forty-five minutes.' He ran his hands lightly along her side, pausing at her breast, rubbing her nipple with his finger until it swelled in ready response. 'You wouldn't believe what could be accomplished in forty-five minutes.'

'I think I could,' Rebecca laughed softly, distracted momentarily from her thoughts as her body slowly filled with the excitement which it appeared he could turn on like a light switch with the smallest of touches.

With the smallest of *looks*. There had been times when he had caught her eye across the room, when Emily's attention had been somewhere else, and just that non-physical contact was always enough to catapult her body into arousal.

If Emily had noticed anything, she had said not a word, which led Rebecca to suspect that she had noticed nothing at all, because restraint was not her middle name. She seemed preoccupied with her own thoughts, and although she still refused to discuss the pregnancy, they both assumed that she was finally thinking about it, coming to terms with its inevitability. She would talk when she was ready.

'Are you sure?' he asked huskily, propping himself on one elbow and leaning towards her so that he could trail a sensuous path across her mouth with his tongue. Rebecca closed her eyes and promptly forgot the serious discussion which she had mentally rehearsed the night before. She lay flat on her back, parting her legs, inviting his hand to slip between them, groaning as his finger rubbed and stroked her wet, swollen bud. Sex with Nicholas Knight had proved to be the most erotic experience she had ever had in her life. She had learned to control her speed, so that her climax, all the more powerful for its delay, coincided with his. It was as though their bodies were meant for one another.

Another delusion, she knew. She tried not to think it, but deep down she knew that he had probably pleasured lots of women in the very same manner. For him, she was a book that was opened many years previously, which he had now had the opportunity to finish. What he was for her was something she deferred thinking about.

'You're beautiful,' he murmured, nibbling her ear, exploring it with his tongue.

'Mm. That feels good.'

'How good?'

'Amazing.' She squirmed against his fingers, moving her hips, then slowing them when the excitement became too much.

'Is my lovemaking the best you've ever had?'

'Mm.'

'What does "Mm" mean?'

'It means that you're good—but why am I telling you this? You probably know that already.'

'But is it the best for *you*?'

She looked at him through half-closed eyes, surprised at the question. 'Does it matter?'

'So it would appear,' he murmured almost inaudibly, using one of her favourite phrases.

'Is that right?' Rebecca laughed lightly. She was no longer an impressionable teenager, and she refused to load his simple statement with meaning. 'Yes, in that case.'

His stiffness jerked against her and she knew that her answer had turned him on. She lightly ran her fingers down his chest, fluttering them against his thigh, and as he groaned she levered herself on to him, riding him slowly. Her breasts hung low and brushed against his mouth and he fastened his lips around her nipple, sucking hard on it.

She had become tuned to his body, could almost feel when his need became greater than his desire for foreplay. She quickened her movements, loving the sensation of her breast in his mouth as she dominated the lovemaking.

Their bodies built up rhythm. His hands were on her hips, pushing her down on him, and their climax was a long, shuddering surrender that happened too quickly, yet not quickly enough.

It sometimes occurred to her that if she had one wish it would be to savour him without any time limits. To make love with him without watching the clock. Not that that diminished the power of their lovemaking. She just wished...

She moved to lie by his side, watching him for a few seconds as he lay with his eyes closed, his breathing still ragged.

'I'll go and have a quick shower,' she said, slipping off the side of the bed and hunting around for the bathrobe which was normally draped over the side of the chair next to her bed. She had lost all inhibitions about making love to him, but for some reason she still felt shy about walking about without any clothes on. She still had a nagging feeling that if he were to look at her without the haze of passion blurring his vision he would find himself making comparisons with all the sexy, slim and probably very compact women he had dated and slept with.

'Don't cover yourself up,' he told her, sitting up on the bed and folding his arms behind his head. 'I've noticed that you always do that. I want to see you without clothes on even when you're not in the act of making love to me.'

Rebecca glanced over her shoulder at him.

'I'm not exactly built like a model,' she laughed nervously, 'more built like a house.'

'Don't.'

'Don't what?' She was still perched on the side of the bed.

'Cry yourself down.'

She stood up and walked nonchalantly across the room, very much conscious of her build. Her body felt wobbly. She was sure that she had gained a thousand pounds in the weeks they had been over here. As she reached the sanctuary of the bathroom and had a very rapid shower, she vowed never to touch another pastry again.

When she emerged, he had already left and she knew that she would find him downstairs in the kitchen, probably reading the French newspaper. It was bizarre. She wondered, briefly, whether the very strangeness of it all amused him. She wondered whether he viewed it as a sort of game, a clandestine game, something novel and exciting that made a change from his normal affairs.

'We need to have a talk.' She released her breath and looked at him as he sat there, cradling a cup of coffee. He had made one for her as well, and she grabbed it up and then sat opposite him.

'Why?' His eyes roved intimately over her and he gave her a long, slow smile.

'Why? Because the holiday's nearly finished and, well, this can't continue.' She had to fight the urge to add, Can it? at the end of the sentence. She had spent the previous night doing very little aside from thinking about where all this was going. It had seemed so wonderfully easy at the beginning, giving in to someone whose brief visit to her life all those years ago had imperceptibly left a stronger mark than she had imagined. They were away from any normal routine and the confinement of their surroundings had worked a magic on her, made her forget a few basic truths which were now rearing their heads as the holiday drew to a close. It was as though the beauty and peace of the surroundings had cast a spell on her.

But Nicholas Knight was still Nicholas Knight. She knew that she turned him on, but she would have been a fool to imagine that it was as straightforward as that. Nicholas Knight was not a straightforward man. His motives would have been complex and there was no doubt whatsoever in her mind that his time with her was little more than a pleasant diversion. He was, after all, as much out of his normal routine as she was. He had told her that he had never felt so relaxed before in his life, that it was as if the frantic world had been slowed down. So was it surprising that, thrown into her company and in the first stages of recovering from the woman he had been seeing for two years, he had turned his attention to her? And found in her a willing participant?

'Why not?' he asked, surprised. 'We've been lovers for almost three weeks now. I've probably talked to you as much as I ever talked to Fiona in all the two years that we were going out.'

'I find that hard to believe,' Rebecca said wryly. 'I may not be the most experienced woman in the world when it comes to relationships with the opposite sex, but I'm not a complete idiot.'

'Why are you sitting on the opposite side of the table?'

he asked suddenly. 'We're back to the teacher/employer scenario, are we?'

'We were always in a teacher/employer scenario.'

'But just with a few additions thrown in.'

'Well, if you want to put it that way.' She knew what she had to do and, while she hoped that he wouldn't make it difficult for her, wouldn't try and persuade her to carry on their affair until it all fizzled out, she found the thought of losing him almost unbearable.

'This is crazy,' he said with suppressed frustration in his voice. 'We want each other; we've been lovers. Why do we suddenly have to start thinking about it? Thinking about the future? Asking lots of questions about whether what we've done is right or wrong or good or bad? What does any of that matter? I'm not kidding when I tell you that I've talked to you more than I ever did to Fiona. We may have dated for two years, but my lifestyle wasn't conducive to a normal relationship.'

'Then why did you maintain the relationship for so long?' Rebecca asked. 'I'm not going to buy into any cheap platitudes, Nicholas. I'm not the teenager you once crossed paths with.'

'Oh, but you are. You might have moved on into the grown-up, responsible arena of teaching, and I know that you're a good teacher. I've watched you at work. Watched how you always manage to get Emily to get her head into her books when someone else might have abandoned all hope in the face of her stubbornness when she's playing up. I've watched the way you patiently go through all her corrections with her in a way that grabs her interest. But underneath it all you're still...delightfully vulnerable and hesitant and endearingly shy.'

This wasn't what she wanted to hear. She didn't want to fight his charm.

'You still haven't said why you and Fiona continued seeing one another for two years if the relationship wasn't...satisfactory.'

'I liked her and it was convenient,' he said bluntly. 'And now I suppose you're going to climb on to your podium and give me a long lecture on men who exploit women, but I can assure you that it was a two-way thing. Fiona was undemanding, fairly irregular company and I liked that. She's a woman who enjoys glitter, a charming bauble on a Christmas tree with none of those feminine yearnings to get inside the kitchen and start the routine of making herself indispensable.'

His mouth tightened involuntarily. 'After Veronica, after her final, desperate act of manipulation to get a wedding band on her finger, I've made sure to stay well away from women who measure relationships in terms of where exactly they're going. You can bet that the minute a woman starts planning a holiday for *next year* she's also started collecting the rope to tie you down.'

He wasn't leaving anything to her imagination, she realised. He had enjoyed himself for the past few weeks and he was happy to continue enjoying himself until such time as he grew bored with her, or else until she began to ask all those nasty, awkward little questions which would have him running for cover as fast as he could. Before she could make the mistake of weaving dreams and anticipating a future, he was telling her that it simply was not going to happen. He was warning her!

And she needed the warning.

With growing horror, she realised that the past few weeks hadn't been a happy, carefree romp in the sack with a man who had fired her senses years ago and had done the same the minute fate had seen fit to throw them together once again. The past few weeks had taken physical attraction and turned it into love. Against all reason, she had fallen in love with Nicholas Knight. She had stupidly convinced herself that her excitement whenever he was around, the images of him that played in her mind in never-ending circles were all to do with sex.

'There's no need for you to tell me all the things you don't want to hear,' she said in a hollow voice. Her hands, cradling the mug, were trembling and she hurriedly removed them and stuck them under her legs. 'I had no intention of trying to make myself indispensable to you. I wouldn't be that stupid! You once asked me why I ran away from you all those years ago. It was because, however gauche and vulnerable you seem to think I am, I was sensible enough to realise that, whatever might have come out of our liaison, it was never going to go the distance.'

'And that was an overnight thought, was it?' He leaned forward and she could tell that the explanation that had dodged him all these years was something he needed to hear.

'I...it was at that party,' she confessed, her stomach tensing as she relived the scene. 'I didn't know anyone there, and you weren't around. I didn't know where you'd gone. I went across to get something to eat and two girls there called me over, asked me who I was. When I told them, one of them said that she'd heard of me, and then she giggled and looked at her friend. It would appear that I was the laughing stock of the place. You'd told everyone that you were bringing an Amazonian country lass to the party, that you intended to have a bit of fun with me but that you'd let them be the judge of whether I was worth it or not.' She could still feel the mortification rise up in her throat like bile, making it hard to swallow. 'I ran away, yes, I'll admit it, but what did you expect me to do? I knew that nothing could come of the two of us anyway,' she shrugged.

'You believed them?' he asked incredulously. He was staring at her as though she had taken leave of her senses. 'You actually believed that nonsense?'

'Why shouldn't I have?'

'Because I would have thought that you knew me, might have given me the chance to deny having said any such thing! Good God. What did these girls look like? Do you remember?'

'How could I forget? They were both quite small. I remember that, even wearing heels, they both had to look up to me. One had very red hair and the other was blonde. A beautiful, tiny blonde girl with great big brown eyes. She was wearing a scarlet and black dress, strapless.' She laughed at herself. 'Crazy the way you remember things.' She looked at him. 'So, you see, there's no chance that I'll ever want anything from you. In fact, I guess I should have hated you when you reappeared in the school, but it had been such a long time and the story was so much more complicated now. You had a daughter! You must have met your ex-wife shortly after I vanished.'

'The blonde one…you're describing Veronica.' He waited as the revelation settled in. 'She must have been jealous as hell of you. You were her competitor, if you'd but known. She must have been in seventh heaven when she found a way of dispatching you.'

They looked at one another, and for some reason they both laughed even though there was nothing very funny about this new version of past events.

'So what I'm saying, Nicholas—' Rebecca sobered up '—is that I wouldn't dream of having any romantic notions about you…' *What a whopper.* 'But I still won't continue with this…this affair, or whatever you care to call it, when we return to England. It's been perfect out here. It's worked for us and it's worked for Emily. She needed the time out to get a grip on her life, but once we're in England things are going to move swiftly. The doctors, the pregnancy will start making more demands on her, the lessons will become more tiring and she will need more and more support to help her face the times that lie ahead. A clandestine affair is just what will *not* be needed.'

'It needn't be clandestine,' he pointed out swiftly. 'I have no qualms about letting Emily—'

'No. It wouldn't be fair on her. She's already got enough on her plate at the moment.'

They looked at one another and the impasse staring at her filled her with a kind of numb dread. Yes, she was being very strong, yes, she was rejecting the one thing she wanted more than anything else in her whole life. But there was no way forward. Every reason she had given him was true, but, more than that, she knew that she could never be satisfied with sex, that sooner or later she would start wanting more, *needing* more. And then where would she be? Past her sell-by date. He had already said as much. Her intellect would start to bore him, her unspoken wants would form a ridge between them and he would edge away as politely but as firmly as he could.

'Fine.' He stood up, and she acknowledged, with disappointment, that he wasn't going to ask twice. Her presence in his life was not important enough for him to try and use his formidable powers of persuasion.

Not, she told herself, that she wanted him to. They had been unfinished chapters in each other's lives, and now their story was over. They would return to England and he would resume his hectic work life and within a couple of months, if that long, he would once again have invited another woman into his life. Another small, glittering

Christmas bauble who made no demands on him intellectually or emotionally.

'So,' he said, halting her before she could slink away to nurse her wounds and convince herself that her moral strength was really far more admirable than merely giving in to passion until it ran its course and left her alone to pick up the pieces. 'Mind telling me what sort of man you have in mind as soulmate and bed companion? If you're that preoccupied with social barriers, then I guess you'll settle into mediocrity with a fellow teacher? Maybe a bank clerk somewhere? Will he have to fill out a questionnaire before he gets a second glance?'

'I'm not…that's not fair… I explained why it would be senseless to carry on with this… We had our fun.'

'Yes, we had our fun,' he agreed, with enough ill humour to lift her spirits.

'Are you looking forward to getting back into the thick of things?'

'I guess that's your not very subtle way of changing the conversation. No, I'm not, as a matter of fact. I've grown rather fond of my leisure time. In fact…' he paused '…I might just start working a bit more from home. I shall certainly cut down my overseas trips. I feel as though I'm making some headway with my daughter. At least she doesn't look at me constantly as though I'm something unfortunate that's crept out of the woodwork. It would be senseless to jeopardise that for the sake of work. As the saying goes, who ever reaches eighty and thanks their lucky stars for the amount of time they've devoted to their work?'

'Quite.' She forced a smile but her mind was furiously working out what exactly he meant by 'working a bit more from home' and cutting down the overseas trips. It would be nice to think that she could cross paths with him on a

daily basis and feel nothing more than relief that she had
had the courage to call it a day. Nice but overly optimistic.
Far more probable was the thought that she would spend
the next few months in a state of constant watchfulness,
having to rein in her wayward emotions and help her cause
by dodging him whenever and however she could. In other
words, live her life in a state of nervous tension.

'I hope that won't pose a problem for you?' he asked,
concerned.

'Why should it?'

'No reason, but you looked a little…dismayed just then
by my suggestion.'

'Obviously it's great that you'll continue the bonding
process with Emily…' Her voice petered out and she tried
to overlay any expression of mounting dismay with a
bright, cheerful, encouraging smile. It made the muscles
in her jaw ache. At the end of her stint with him, she
foresaw a lifelong problem with screwed-up facial muscles
from the effort of smiling too much and high blood pressure from the effort of coping with the ongoing battle between her head and her emotions.

'I'm so pleased to hear you agree with me,' he said,
laying it on thick but maintaining enough of a concerned
countenance to stir up thoughts of physical violence in her.
'I wouldn't want to make life uncomfortable for you in
any way.' To her suspicious ears, it sounded as though
what he planned was to make life as uncomfortable for her
as he possibly could. 'In fact, I won't be in your way at
all during the day.'

She allowed herself a small sigh of relief. Perhaps she
had been misreading him.

'When I work from home, you won't know I'm in the
house. Occasionally, I might break the day with lunch
somewhere.' He appeared to give this idea some thought.

'Somewhere cheap and cheerful. You and Emily will probably enjoy the break as well.'

The small window of relief vanished and was replaced by alarm.

'And, of course, I shall still have to do some client entertaining at night.'

Oh, good, she thought as the rollercoaster took her on another small upward slope.

'But I shall severely limit them. I've found that my deputies have done a damn good job in my absence. In fact, it's probably done them a world of good having their boss out of sight for a while. I don't know about you, but I've always had a problem with delegation. If there's something to be done, I've always been convinced that I'm the only one who could handle it. But I've now come to the conclusion that that sort of proprietorial attitude can end up stunting other people's talent. Yes...' He rubbed his chin thoughtfully and she got the impression that he was thoroughly enjoying himself. The sadist. 'It's been quite an eye-opener for me in more ways than one.'

'Grand!' Rebecca said weakly.

'I might even be able to devote myself to a few pet projects I've been contemplating for some time now but putting off because of pressure of work. Isn't it incredible the way life rushes by and you don't even realise it at the time?'

'Incredible.'

'Sometimes you just need to force yourself to slow down.'

'But not too slow,' she pointed out quickly. 'Nothing worse than a fine brain stagnating through lack of use!'

'Oh, that won't be a problem with me. Anyway, we shall have lots of opportunities to discuss that theory and many others over dinner in the evenings. Mrs Dunne will be in

her element having a full house to cater for.' He seemed
thoroughly satisfied with his future arrangements. 'Now
that we've settled all this, shall we meander down to the
town and rescue Emily just in case she forgets her time
limit?'

'Good idea.'

They wrapped themselves up and walked slowly down
to the town. Hopefully, they would meet Emily returning;
there was only one clear road back to the farmhouse. But
naturally no such luck. Not that Nicholas seemed bothered
by her company. He chatted amicably for the duration of
the walk, unperturbed by her lack of enthusiasm.

Why was he doing this? Why was he tormenting her?
Underneath the thoughtful exterior, she knew damn well
that he was fully aware of the effect his continual presence
would have on her. He *knew* that the prospect of a nightly
dinner with him and Emily, not to mention *occasional
lunches out*, 'somewhere cheap and cheerful', threw her
into a state of panic and confusion, so why had he taken
such delight in suggesting it?

She didn't bother him the way he bothered her. Was it
his twisted way of making her pay for breaking off the
relationship before he was ready to be through with it? She
glanced across at the tall, dark-haired man striding along-
side her, the easy assurance of his walk, the slight smile
playing on his lips, and felt a rush of hot resentment.

She didn't know what reaction she had expected from
him to her decision to call the whole thing off, but if he
had had an ounce of consideration he would have instantly
made plans to make himself scarce at least while she was
still on the premises.

With fatalistic resignation, she realised that she just had
not thought ahead far enough. She should have reasonably
foreseen that he would have continued to make headway

with Emily by being around more for her, but, she thought with frustration, he could have had the decency to exclude her from the scenario.

She was simmering by the time they reached the town. If he launched into any more cool, adult conversation pieces on the delights of châteaux, fortresses and the River Loire, she would lunge.

'Where do you think she'll be?' he asked, frowning and looking around for inspiration. 'I thought we'd have passed her on the way down.'

'We could try the café,' Rebecca suggested, which they duly did. Fruitlessly.

'Well, we have to locate her,' Nicholas said, after a few more fruitless visits to obvious shops. 'She doesn't have a key to let herself into the house and I don't intend to spend the rest of the day hunting for Emily and missing her by a few seconds. We'll have to split up and meet back here in…' he consulted his watch '…half an hour.'

Before she could say anything, he headed off in the opposite direction, walking slowly and peering through windows, and after a few seconds Rebecca veered off towards the narrower streets with their sprinkling of seventeenth- and eighteenth-century houses, liberally interlaced with cafés and bars, where splendid wine could be bought for a fraction of the price they would pay in England.

She didn't know what made her pause outside one of the more intimate bars along the street. It wasn't open, but a flicker of movement caught her eye and as she peered into the bowels of the place she let out a gasp of surprise.

Emily! Laughing with a young man who was getting things ready behind the wooden counter.

She banged on the door, making sure that they couldn't see her through the window, and kept banging until she heard locks being undone, then she stormed in and confronted Emily, who seemed shell-shocked by the sudden apparition of her teacher in fury.

'What is going on here?' Rebecca boomed, satisfied to see that they were both cringing at her tone of voice.

The lad, with a teacloth draped over one shoulder, looked no older than eighteen. He was tall and slim and good-looking in an innocent, boyish kind of way. He launched into an explanation in rapid French and Rebecca held up one imperious hand to halt him in mid-flow.

'What do you have to say for yourself, *young lady*?'

Emily was staring at her mutinously, but her guilt was sufficient to make her launch into a frantic explanation of events. It wasn't the way it looked. Pierre was just a good friend. They had met accidentally in the café and she had been seeing him to chat, *to practise her French*, for the past few weeks. To practise her French! Rebecca nearly burst out laughing. But this was a serious situation. Had Emily learnt nothing at all from what had happened to her? Was the child a complete nitwit?

'You won't tell Dad, will you?' Emily pleaded, her eyes filling up. Her slender fingers clutched Rebecca's coat sleeve, as though unwilling to let her go until the question had been answered.

'He's looking for you,' Rebecca said darkly. Heaven help her if he found her here. Thank God he had beaten a path in the opposite direction. It didn't take a genius to work out what his reaction would be to this cosy little sight of his daughter ensconced in a dark French tavern with a good-looking young boy. *Good friends* and *someone to practise French on* were two explanations he would not buy in a month of Sundays.

'Please!' Emily sobbed. 'He'll kill me and I wasn't doing anything wrong. I swear!'

Rebecca hesitated. 'Let's go right now,' she said

sharply. 'I'm not promising to cover for you, but you and I will have a serious little chat when we get back. About *everything*. Is that clear?'

'Yes!' Emily closed her eyes with relief. 'I need to talk to you; there are a few things that…'

Neither of them saw Nicholas until he was virtually towering over them, his face a study in thunderous rage. Pierre, who had obviously guessed that he was witnessing a very uncomfortable, private domestic scene of biblical proportions, had tactfully disappeared through the door behind the counter.

'So here you are!' He looked from one to the other. 'What the hell are you doing here?' His voice was deceptively quiet and all the more terrifying for it.

'Let's just take a minute to calm down,' Rebecca began.

'You *said* it was all right for me to come to town on my own for a couple of hours a day!'

'Not to a bar!' His head swung around and he caught a glimpse of the hapless Pierre in the back room. 'With a man!'

'He's only seventeen!'

'That's not the point!'

'We just spent the time *talking*!'

'A likely story! Do you really expect us to believe that?'

'I believe her,' Rebecca said quietly, which drew a look of gratitude from Emily and one of rage from her father.

'And if you think that two females sticking together is going to work then you're both in for a shock!' The quiet voice had risen a few decibels. 'Have you got a brain in your head, Emily? Do you *remember* why you got expelled from school?'

'Stop shouting at me!' she shouted tearfully.

'Stop shouting at you? You should be grateful that I'm

not throttling you! What the hell do you think you're playing at?'

Pierre had emerged nervously from his hiding place and was attempting to intercede in what he presumably thought was World War Three in the making, only to be summarily dismissed by Nicholas.

'I'm not playing at anything!'

'Hasn't the pregnancy done anything to dampen your *high spirits*?' He looked suddenly bewildered and disappointed and Emily gave a choked little sob.

'I...I...I've got something to say to you...to you both,' she whispered, wringing her hands together. 'I've wanted to say something sooner, but...' She looked wildly at Rebecca for help and Rebecca grasped one of her fluttering hands and stilled it within her own.

'Shouting at Emily isn't going to help matters along,' she told Nicholas coldly. 'If she has something to tell us, then I suggest we sit down and hear her out.'

At last, she thought, Emily was going to face her past and come to terms with it with her father.

CHAPTER NINE

'WE'LL go back to the house,' Nicholas said in a clipped voice, turning away.

'No! I want to stay here,' Emily told them. Her voice was shaky, and Rebecca noticed that as she spoke she glanced surreptitiously around the bar, seeking out Pierre, who inclined his head slightly in a reassuring gesture.

'You'll do as I say, my girl,' Nicholas said grimly, and Rebecca, catching his eye, glared at him. The man was mad. Did he think that he was going to help things along if he adopted this high-handed, arrogant, paternalistic attitude? 'Well, I don't suppose it matters where the hell we go,' he conceded, glaring back at Rebecca. 'Get the boy to sort out something to drink.'

Emily called something to him in French, and they moved across to one of the tables, removing the chairs which had been placed upside down on the top, setting them out, then they awkwardly positioned themselves like three people about to conduct a heated argument on a contentious subject. Which, Rebecca thought, they were.

Nicholas was finding it difficult to meet his daughter's eye. He sat rigidly in the wooden chair, arms folded, expression unyielding.

They had covered so much distance in the past few weeks. Why had Emily chosen to shoot herself in the foot by doing the one thing guaranteed to send her father into a blind fury? There was something pathetically innocent and horrendously stupid about meeting a young French lad

at a sensitive time like this, when solitude should have
been her chosen route.

How ironic to think that she and Nicholas had congratulated themselves on how successfully Emily was dealing
with her problems. They had cheerfully concluded that her
time spent away from the house and away from the constant reminder of why she was in France in the first place
had done her a world of good. They couldn't have been
further from the truth. She had used the opportunity to do
precisely what she had done in England.

Rebecca felt sick with guilt. If, if, if. If they had not
been having an affair of their own, would they have been
as willing to allow her that small taste of freedom? Most
probably, but at the end of the day it had suited them both.

Whatever revelation Emily would spring on them, it was
little consolation that the biggest one had already been
sprung. She was already pregnant. What could be worse?

A new thought formed in Rebecca's head, took shape
and, as three mugs of frothy coffee were deposited by the
alarmed and sheepish Pierre, grew to its full, devastating
potential.

What if Emily had lied to the boy about her age? What
if they had secretly married? Was that possible? No, she
told herself logically. But Emily had something to say and,
whatever it was, it was scaring the life out of her. Her eyes
kept skittering towards her father and skittering away, and
her hands, as she lifted the mug of coffee to her lips, were
trembling so much that some of the hot liquid spilled, and
she slowly replaced the mug on its saucer.

'Don't be afraid, Emily,' she said gently, ignoring
Nicholas's granite expression. One look at his face made
minced meat of her reassurances, and Emily bit her bottom
lip anxiously.

'Dad?' she said timidly, and he looked at her with steely-eyed coldness.

'I can't begin to tell you how disappointed I am in you,' he began.

'Good. Then spare us all,' Rebecca snapped. Their eyes met and she coolly outstared him until he retreated into a ferocious silence.

'I don't know how to say this,' Emily mumbled miserably. 'I wanted to tell you sooner, but I couldn't.'

'Tell us what?' Rebecca tried a smile, a motherly, comforting smile, and was rewarded with a tentative relaxation of hunched shoulders.

'I'm not pregnant.'

Three little words. They danced in the air like some dizzy, unbelievable tune that had the power to move mountains.

Nicholas was staring at his daughter at last with a stunned expression. 'What?'

'I'm not pregnant. I lied.' Her voice was almost inaudible and Rebecca found herself straining forward to hear her.

'I don't understand...' she said, utterly bewildered. 'Is this some kind of sick joke, Emily?'

'No joke.' Relief to be telling the truth at last gave her voice more authority. 'I lied about the pregnancy. I did it because I hated the boarding-school. I didn't want to go there. I *never* wanted to go there. I felt as though I was being shunted off to make life more convenient for Dad and Fiona and I hated it so much. I'd had loads of freedom in Australia, and although Mum was hell a lot of the time at least I wasn't cooped up. I felt as though I was caught in some terrible trap. You didn't want to know me, Dad, so you just packed me off to the furthest spot you could come up with because I disrupted your life and your routine!' Her voice now was strong and accusatory.

'You never said anything about feeling this way at the time,' Nicholas retorted.

'How could I? I'm not a wimp!'

'You could have confided in one of the teachers,' Rebecca said, shaken.

'Who? There was no one! I guess I thought that if I behaved badly enough I'd get myself kicked out, but it never worked. You were all so *sympathetic*.' The little voice that had been buried for years began to rise to the surface.

'I'm not a mind-reader,' Nicholas said gruffly. 'You should have said something.'

'Every time you were around, Fiona was there as well! Anyway, I saw this movie on telly and it gave me the idea. So I made the whole thing up. I didn't think about all the trouble I would cause. I just did it to get out of the school. I figured that once I was out I'd explain everything and it would be all right.'

The naïvety of youth, Rebecca thought. For a clever girl like Emily, her mind had moved in a mysteriously simple way if she hadn't foreseen the consequences of her actions.

'Why didn't you?' Rebecca asked curiously. 'You could have admitted the truth over the Christmas holidays.'

'I never got the chance, and then you came and suddenly something right happened for once. Fiona vanished from the scene.' Even at a time like this, she was young enough to allow a smile of pleasure to cross her lips. Nicholas, noticing it, shook his head wonderingly, and for the first time Rebecca could see the father in him, shaking his head at incomprehensibly bad behaviour which he was about to forgive.

'I never knew you disliked her that much,' he interjected.

'Because she was loathsome,' Emily told him, as though that simple fact spoke for itself. 'Every chance she got, she told me, smiling all the while, how awkward my presence was.'

'So you didn't say a word. You maintained the lie. Why?' Rebecca frowned.

'Well, you'd arrived on the scene, and I could tell that Dad was interested in you.' Now that she had jumped the highest hurdle and was still in one piece, she was confident enough to grin at Rebecca's mounting colour at her observation.

'D-don't be silly,' Rebecca stammered. Under the table, she felt Nicholas's foot against hers, a subtle pressure, just enough to remind her of their lovemaking.

'Dad's a different person when he's with you,' Emily said with childish enthusiasm. 'He doesn't bellow at me.'

'I *never* bellowed at you.' He cleared his throat uncomfortably. 'Well, hardly ever. You deserved it a lot of the time! You can be a little minx when you put your mind to it!'

'I was going to tell you over here, I swear I was, but things were going so good and I didn't want to spoil it.' Her voice was wistful. 'I felt like you were noticing me for the first time. You asked me about my work. You even helped me when I got stuck with the physics.' There was open yearning in the voice now that made Rebecca want to weep.

'Actually, I'm very good at physics,' Nicholas said roughly. 'And I enjoyed it,' he mumbled, looking away.

Pierre, now sensing that World War Three had been diverted, had emerged from behind the counter with a refill of coffee and a beaming smile on his face. With relief,

Rebecca saw that he was sensible enough not to try his luck by entering the conversation, however. He poured the coffee, winked at Emily when he thought that the adults weren't looking, and retired to a slightly more prominent position behind the counter.

'And then I felt an atmosphere between the two of you.'

'An atmosphere?' Rebecca and Nicholas said in guilty unison, and Emily nodded slowly.

'Like you two were checking each other out when you thought I wouldn't notice.'

Wild colour crawled up Rebecca's neckline to her cheeks. She wondered if, with a mammoth effort of will, she might evaporate.

'So I kind of put off telling you and decided to give you a bit of space.'

For the first time ever, Nicholas appeared lost for words, as though he was desperately trying to work out the mechanism of his daughter's brain and failing.

'You decided to give *us* a bit of space,' he repeated.

'Yes. Dad, I know you won't believe me but you've mellowed. Then I met Pierre.' She tensed up again and held her breath in anticipation of a lecture that failed to be delivered. Nicholas just sat there in fairly stunned silence. 'I told him everything. He's been a real mate to me.' She flashed Pierre a radiant smile and he smiled back eagerly. 'I guess I just slipped into a kind of nice, comfortable routine,' she finished lamely. 'Are you still mad at me? Do you hate me?'

'You confound me. *Women* confound me!' He threw up his hands helplessly. 'And no, I'm not still mad at you. I'm bloody overjoyed if you want the truth. And no, I don't hate you and I never did. I...'

He didn't have time to complete the sentence because Emily threw herself at him in a huge hug and after a second's surprise he returned the hug, stroking her hair. When she finally pulled away, his face was dark and he was trying hard to conceal his delight. Trying but not quite succeeding because he smiled broadly and shook his head again.

'Well, I think I need a stiff drink after all this,' he said, standing up and slipping back on his heavy trench coat. He wagged his finger at Emily. 'And you, my girl, will stay here and finish practising your French with the boy and will return home in one hour.'

Rebecca wished that she could catch the utter joy that spread across Emily's face and bottle it for ever. She stood up as well and stuck on her own battered waterproof.

They decided, by mutual unspoken agreement, not to return to the house immediately but to stroll through the village for a short while. The sun was bright and it was a relatively mild day, too cold for a mere jumper but not so cold that being outdoors was inconceivable.

'Well, what do you make of all that?' Nicholas asked as they paused and looked into the shop windows and then automatically headed for their usual café. 'What a spectacular lie. I should be as mad as hell at the chaos she managed to cause but I'm so relieved. No wonder she never wanted to discuss the pregnancy!'

'Quite,' Rebecca said wryly. 'And to think that I put it down to denial. It's finally convinced me that a career in psychotherapy isn't for me.' Faced with this sudden shock, the coldness between them had disappeared, but she knew that that was only a temporary blip for them.

'You have to admit that the girl's imaginative,' he said, with a certain amount of grudging admiration and pride.

'That she is, although…' They had reached the café and he pushed open the door, stepping aside to let her through. Rebecca felt her body brush lightly against his and she had to fight down her automatic response to the brief physical contact.

'Although…?' he asked.

Their faces were now so well-known at the café that they no longer needed to signal for the waitress. She automatically appeared, with a smile on her face. They ordered two *café au laits* and a couple of enormous pastries which Rebecca decided to eat without guilt because it had been, so far, an extraordinary day.

'Although…' she leaned forward and rested her elbows on the table '…if she had said something sooner, she might have spared me the exercise of coming down here in the first place.'

At that, his face tightened. 'Of course,' he told her, his mouth twisting. 'Why hadn't I considered that?'

'I didn't mean that the way it sounded,' Rebecca rushed on uncomfortably. She bit into the pastry as an excuse to win a little time to gather her thoughts together, and watched as the crumbs flew around the plate and adhered inelegantly to her mouth. She licked them away, then wiped her lips with her napkin, aware that he was watching every little movement.

'It's just that…I *have* taken a certain amount of time off work and they *have* found a replacement to cover for me in my absence.' When she saw that he was looking at her as though any such consideration was hardly worth talking about, she felt a little spurt of anger. 'This may seem trivial to you,' she snapped, 'but it leaves me with a problem of what I do for the remainder of the year! Emily will now be eligible once again for school—a *day* school somewhere local—and I shall be left twiddling my thumbs and falling back on my savings to make ends meet until I can recommence work at the boarding-school!'

'If it's just a question of money…'

'It is *not* just a question of money! Even if you offered me the full year's worth of salary, I wouldn't dream of taking it! Do you imagine that my pride would stand for that?'

'Perish the thought,' he said harshly. 'I've seen for myself that your pride stands for very little, but a halo can become a very heavy burden even if you *do* have five minutes of self-righteous bliss every evening when you take it off to shine it!'

'I'm sorry if you think that having one or two principles is the equivalent of wearing a burdensome halo on my head!'

'Your so-called principles were conspicuously absent over the past three weeks!' he bit back, and she flinched at the verbal blow. As if she hadn't faced that painful realisation herself already! As if she hadn't faced the anguished truth that she had fallen in love with the man! Did he have to rub it in? Yes, she thought, of course he did. His masculine pride had been wounded because he had been denied what he wanted!

'Anyway,' he said, breaking the tense silence, 'you're contracted to give me a month's notice.'

'And you intend to make me work it out?' Rebecca asked incredulously.

'You're not going to leave Emily in the lurch to suit yourself,' he said savagely, his eyes cold.

'I'm sure you could arrange for her to be taken immediately into one of the schools. They would be sympathetic to—'

'Under no circumstances. You'll work your notice.'

'But *why*?' she asked, bewildered, appealing for him to see sense. Why would he possibly want her to be around when their relationship had ended and being in each other's company could only serve to remind them both of the fact?

She soon found out when, the following day, they arrived back in England to the dreary wet skies they had left behind a few weeks previously.

Thankfully, she had sat next to Emily so that Nicholas could spread his paperwork across both seats and Emily was enough of a distraction for Rebecca to put what was on her mind temporarily to the back burner. Her thoughts were still there, waiting like an itch to be scratched, and, much as she dreaded the prospect of morbid analysis of what had happened, she knew that she could not avoid it.

As soon as they had landed and cleared through Customs, Nicholas turned to them and warmly told Emily that he had to go to work but that he would be back in time for dinner.

For Rebecca he reserved a curt nod, and as soon as he had walked away and been absorbed by the crowds Emily, restrained in her observations about them thus far, turned to Rebecca and said, without preamble, 'So what's eating him?'

'These crowds! I'd forgotten how exhausting it can be over here! That's what one month in rural France does for a girl, wouldn't you agree?' She positioned herself in the queue for taxis and did her best to appear anxious and distracted.

'You haven't answered my question,' Emily persisted. 'Why is Dad in such a foul mood?'

'Is he? I hadn't noticed.' Mild surprise. That was the intention. Instead, she heard her voice reverberate with guilty acknowledgement. She would never make an actress.

'Yes, you have,' Emily accused. 'Have you two had a

row?'

'Don't be silly, Emily,' Rebecca dismissed firmly, shuffling along in the freezing cold as the queue moved forwards.

'I'm not being silly and stop treating me like a child.' At last, a taxi. They shuffled in and, after giving the driver the address, Rebecca rested against the seat, closed her eyes and prayed that Emily wouldn't persist in her cross-examination. She could, she knew, simply refuse to answer any questions, but then that would be suspicious in itself. On the other hand, if she *did* answer, she was a dreadful liar.

'What transpired between your father and myself is not important,' she said. 'The main thing is that you can return to mainstream education at the start of the summer term.'

'Ah, so something *did* transpire between you and Dad. I knew it! I could tell. All those fishy sidelong looks and being cooped up in that romantic little stone farmhouse every day for hours on end.'

Rebecca's eyes flew open. 'You're being ridiculous and imaginative!'

'No, I'm not,' Emily said stubbornly. 'I'm not blind and I'm not an idiot. You and Dad really hit it off, didn't you?' Her voice was thick with inflection and she refused to wither under Rebecca's warning glare. Like father, like daughter.

'Emily, I'm too tired to discuss any of this. None of it *matters* anyway.'

That bought her a moment's reprieve. Emily stared vacantly out of the window for a few seconds, then made some gloomy remarks about London. She missed that little farmhouse, she said wistfully, which Rebecca loosely translated as missing the sweet-faced Pierre.

'And now you and Dad have had some kind of blazing argument, which means that things are going to be really uncomfortable for me again.'

'You,' Rebecca said, unable to resist a grin, 'are a little devil.'

'I'm not!' But the protestation was delivered with a very pink face. 'I just want to know what's going on! I'm an adult now. I know I'm not pregnant, but I *could* have been.'

'I fail to see the logic of that argument.'

'And you're just trying to get rid of me by changing the subject. Why won't you tell me what's going on? So you and Dad had a fling. Do you think I'm going to be shocked by that?' Emily wore a smug expression on her face when she said that. 'Why did you have a row?'

'Oh, stop,' Rebecca said wearily. 'It's not going to get you anywhere. If you're that interested, then you should ask your father for details.'

'As if!'

'Well, then, can we just drop it?'

'Sure.' She shrugged casually and smoothed her black woollen skirt with the flat of her hand. It was fairly short when she was standing up, and sitting down seemed to reduce it to the size of a handkerchief. No wonder the hapless Pierre had seemed so besotted with her. She had the same sort of casual, unconscious elegance that her father possessed, the same striking combination of stunning good looks and intelligence. In Emily, the two were not yet fully formed, but in a few years' time she would be a daunting prospect for any man. The sort of girl who would not be afraid to speak her mind with the self-confidence born of physical beauty.

'But sometimes it does help to talk,' Emily said in a

sweetly sympathetic voice. So sweetly sympathetic that Rebecca burst out laughing.

'I'll bear that in mind,' she said, sobering up but still wearing a wide smile on her face.

In fact, she very nearly telephoned her best friend Amy as soon as she got back, but then the entire episode seemed so convoluted that she abandoned the idea and spent the remainder of the day nursing her private thoughts.

Talking to someone would not ease matters anyway. In fact, she suspected that if she started pouring her heart out she would end up blubbing. To be hurt once by a man was a mistake. To be hurt again by the same man years later struck Rebecca as out-and-out stupidity. There had been a thousand warning signs and she had blithely disregarded them all, convinced that she was smart enough not to let her heart get involved with the antics of her body. She had managed to persuade herself that because she was no longer young and naïve she must be older and wiser. What folly. The fact was that she might not be as young or as naïve as she once was, but when it came to Nicholas Knight she was anything but older and wiser.

As seven-thirty rolled around, she began to feel her stomach twist into knots. The thought of lurking upstairs in her bedroom with the excuse of having a headache or being terminally exhausted was tempting, but she suspected that he would just barge into the bedroom and insist that she sit down for dinner with them. She had delivered a blow to his ego, and he was determined to make her pay for it. Either that or he was so supremely indifferent to her company that he was quite unaware of the potential for awkwardness.

At seven forty-five, she reluctantly dragged herself to the sitting room to find that it wasn't to be the party of three which she had been dreading. It was to be a party of four, because he had invited a guest to dinner. A young, nubile, frothy red-haired beauty who smiled a great deal and seemed inordinately bowled over by Nicholas's forceful presence. Emily, after a moment's hesitation, during which time her eyes slid thoughtfully from Rebecca to her father, then back to Rebecca, adapted to the situation with good grace. She chatted about fashion and pop groups, none of which Rebecca had ever heard of, but then Emily would only have been a few years younger than her father's new playmate.

It was the most uncomfortable evening of her life. The food tasted like cardboard, she was back to feeling Amazonian and inelegant and she found the thought of Nicholas in bed with the small redhead physically sickening.

She couldn't wait for the evening to draw to a close, but when, after her rushed cup of coffee, she stood up to excuse herself Nicholas, who had had far too much to drink, waved her back down peremptorily.

'Where you goin'?' he asked with the threat of belligerence in his voice.

Emily, surprisingly, seemed amused by her father's inebriation.

'To bed,' Rebecca said politely, before going through the usual 'very nice to meet you's with Chloe.

'Just the place I'd like to be,' he said loudly, giving his playmate a warm, knowing look, and Rebecca clamped her teeth firmly together.

'Then you should watch what you drink,' Rebecca said icily. 'I'm sure Chloe would be very disappointed if you collapsed in a stupor the minute you got there.' With which she walked out of the room, her head held high, and as soon as she reached the stairs and was safely out of sight she ran up them, two at a time, her heart beating hard from a combination of jealousy, anger and sheer misery.

The following morning she sneaked downstairs to the kitchen, well after nine-thirty, leaving Emily in the upstairs office with her usual workload, to find Nicholas lounging in front of the newspaper, cup of coffee in one hand and seemingly in no rush to get himself off to work.

'So you're up at last!' he said heartily, lowering the newspaper to eye her over the top of it. 'Emily and I ate breakfast about an hour ago.'

The little traitor had said not a word about her father still being in the house, Rebecca thought with irritation.

'I had no idea that I'm required to have breakfast with you as well,' she said coolly, reaching to get herself a mug and then filling it with some of the coffee from the pot. No, she was *not* going to scrutinise him for signs of over-night wear and tear. What he did in his bed from now on, and with whom, was entirely his own business.

'Just as long as you're not slacking off.' He gave an indolent shrug of his shoulders. 'I've seen this syndrome before. Employee hands in notice and works the statutory month, during which time they do as little as possible in as many ways as they can think how.'

'I am not *slacking off*,' Rebecca said heatedly.

'You can sit at the kitchen table, you know. No need to hover over there as though you're on the brink of taking flight. I don't bite.'

She could feel the colour in her cheeks at that remark and was angry with herself because she knew that that was his intention. She sidled to a chair, sat down and swallowed some of the coffee, which was tepid and disgusting.

'Feeling all right?' he asked in a concerned tone of voice. 'You look a little off colour this morning.' He paused to stroke his chin thoughtfully with one finger.

'Come to think of it, you seemed a little jaded last night as well.'

'I've never felt better in my life before.'

'And what did you think of Chloe?' He smiled a little half-smile to himself and she could have flung the cup at his head. Instead, she clutched it a little tighter, only loosening her grip when she realised that she was at risk of shattering it into a thousand pieces. 'A gorgeous little butterfly, wouldn't you say? And so unassuming as well. Quite remarkable, considering her…physical assets…' He let his voice trail away into suggestive silence.

'She seemed very *young*. Could almost be a friend of Emily's, in fact!' The slight darkening of his skin was enough to give her a bit of momentum. 'Isn't there some kind of law involving minors?'

'She happens to be twenty.'

'So just out of adolesence. That's all right, then!'

The suggestive little smile that had tugged at his mouth had now blossomed into a scowl.

'But she *is* very decorative,' Rebecca continued in a placatory voice, and was masochistically pleased when he abruptly stood up, shoved the newspaper into his briefcase and informed her that he had to go.

'But I'll be back for dinner tonight,' he said silkily. 'So I'll see you both later.' He snapped shut the briefcase and strode out of the kitchen, leaving Rebecca to wonder whether she had won anything just then.

It didn't feel like it when the day progressed in fairly similar lines to the previous day. She was distracted, absent-minded and had to force a smile on her face whenever she caught Emily staring at her.

'She doesn't *mean* anything to him, you know,' Emily confided in a whisper, after Rebecca had corrected her day's work and had gone through the task of pointing out her mistakes. 'Shall I tell you what I reckon?'

'No.'

'*I* reckon that he just brought that bimbo along last night to make you jealous! His eyes were all over you when you weren't looking!'

Were they? She felt a little thrill of pleasure which she deadened with a swift jab of common sense.

At seven-thirty, she proceeded with rather more caution to the sitting room and was relieved to find only Nicholas and Emily present. He was glaring, she was smiling and they both stopped talking as soon as she walked into the room.

'I was just telling Dad—'

'About schools,' he interrupted tersely, his eyes swooping over Rebecca with ill-humoured intensity. 'Day schools in the area.'

'I can make a few calls in the morning,' Rebecca said, sitting down and giving her skirt a swift tug so that it exposed less thigh. 'Maybe we can arrange some appointments to view a few.' She smiled at Emily, aware that Nicholas's expression hadn't lightened.

'I think I should come along and have a look as well,' he said heavily, 'just in case you're thinking of eliminating me from the equation.'

'I wasn't thinking any such thing!'

'Dad's in a foul mood because I've told him that I refuse to sit through another evening socialising with another bimbo,' Emily said, apropos of nothing in particular.

'*Another* bimbo?' She felt that familiar lurch in her gut, very similar to the one that had afflicted her the evening before when she had seen the 'butterfly' Chloe.

'Yes…' Emily drew breath to explain.

'Look, I cancelled the woman,' Nicholas grated. 'Let's

just leave it at that, shall we? I'm sure Rebecca doesn't want to be bored to death by a lengthy explanation of who said what and why.' He fidgeted and shot her a dark, brooding look. 'Anyway, Lolly isn't a bimbo. She just happens to be a very talented financial consultant.'

'Lolly?' Rebecca asked in amazement.

'Her nickname. Don't ask me why.' He shrugged and tossed her a sudden, wicked grin which made her mouth tighten.

Which rendered the evening another nightmare of wild imaginings. First Chloe. Then Lolly. Had he decided to go through a parade of youthful beauties just to prove that she, Rebecca, had been but a number in the barrel, despite the fact that she had been the one to terminate their affair?

Over a fine meal of salmon and new potatoes, served with regimented precision by Mrs Dunne, who was clearly in her element despite the pursed lips and the exaggerated shakes of the head if so much as a cauliflower floret was left uneaten on a plate, Rebecca fulminated silently about the absent Lolly. By the time coffee rolled round, she was almost sorry that the mysterious Lolly had not made an appearance. Her presence might at least have put her out of her misery.

But the threat of Lolly did not last long. One night, in fact. Because over the next three weeks she was subjected to several other girls, all young, all beautiful, all tiny. And when there was none she still had to sit through dinner with Nicholas and Emily and force herself to make polite conversation.

The only light on the horizon was the fact that Emily and Nicholas appeared to have jumped a hurdle and were communicating at long last. They had finally broken the ice and spoken to one another about the past which had hung between them like a silent wall of steel.

And a school had been found. The three of them had traipsed around several, and in the end had narrowed the choice to one. Emily would start at the beginning of the summer term.

Now, with the prospect of departure looming in less than a week, Rebecca sat on the bed and contemplated her future. She had reassured Emily that she would keep in touch, and of course she would, provided Nicholas was nowhere on the scene. If she had learnt anything at all over the past three weeks, it was that in a relationship, out of a relationship, the man was dangerous to her health. His simply being somewhere in the vicinity threw her into a state of anguished confusion.

Although he still watched her, his eyes savage and brooding, he had recovered from what she had done. He had been able to throw himself back into his social whirl as though she had been nothing but a passing ripple.

She dragged her suitcase out of the cupboard and bitterly began to pack to go back home.

Where she belonged.

CHAPTER TEN

WHERE *did* she belong?

Nearly three weeks on and Rebecca still felt miserably out of sync. It had been a painful parting. Surprisingly so. Emily had struggled to maintain a brave face, but her eyes had been glistening as she had waved Rebecca off in the taxi. With heart-wrenching short-sightedness, she had somehow expected Rebecca to stay on, even though the thought had not been put into words. Rebecca knew that much of Emily's desolation was due to the fact that somewhere, in the recesses of her brain, she had linked Rebecca to the start of good relations between her father and herself and to the disappearance of Fiona.

'You *will* keep in touch, won't you?' she had pleaded, and Rebecca, having promised, had been true to her word. She had spoken to Emily twice a week since she had left, and it had taken an enormous effort not to linger over mention of Nicholas and certainly not to be drawn into any dubious questions about whether she was missed.

She wasn't.

In fact, she had not even seen him on the morning of her departure. He had spoken to her the evening before, a brief, indifferent conversation during which he'd thanked her for all she had done and all that she had been prepared to do. There had been no references to their short fling. That entire episode seemed to have slipped into history as far as he was concerned. He had barely looked at her and Rebecca had left with the impression that every word that had crossed his lips had been a mere concession to politeness, something to be endured before he rushed ahead with more important business. More than anything else, that had hurt.

He had insisted, riding over all her protests, that he pay her for the full duration of her contract, even though she was leaving early, and now she was forced to admit that it did make things easier. Her room at the boarding-school was no longer available, but at least she could afford to rent a house without thinking of the cost, and in the past couple of weeks she had tentatively been to a few estate agents with a view to buying.

She had no intention of moving back into residence at the boarding-school, even though the place had been offered back to her when she recommenced work there in the following January. She felt as though she had spent far too long stagnating.

All those years during which she had thrown herself into her teaching career, proudly sitting back every so often to view her accomplishments, now seemed like the useless activity of a gerbil frantically turning circles on its little wheel, moving quickly but going nowhere.

Nicholas Knight had come thundering into her life and now, without him, everything seemed vaguely meaningless.

Next week would be better, she told herself firmly. She would be starting a fill-in job at the local state school and she would start making arrangements for a mortgage. Two properties to view in the coming week, one of which she had fallen in love with from the picture alone.

She stared without enthusiasm at the gathering dusk and at the first signs of spring appearing outside in the front garden and told herself that everything on the horizon looked positively brilliant.

She was in limbo at the moment, she decided, and as

soon as life started moving again she would stop dwelling on Nicholas and churning over in her mind all those memories which she had obviously been storing subconsciously for just such a time as this, when they could return with force to beat her about the head. She would be just too busy to linger over him. Teaching at a new school, buying a house—these were things that would distract her.

On the spur of the moment, she telephoned Emily, hoping that Nicholas would not be home and yet longing to hear his voice, longing so much that it became a physical pain.

'Hi, Emily. Rebecca here.'

'No need to sound so disappointed.' Emily sounded as though she was speaking on a line from the next room. Her voice was loud and clear.

'How's the new school?'

'Great. Uniform sucks but the school's pretty good. Course, I've already clocked on to a couple of teachers who could do with a small rehaul, but don't worry—' she laughed '—I don't intend to put them to the test. You should come back here and teach, you know. It's a lot livelier in London. Dad says...'

'Dad says...what?' She could hear the sudden tension in her voice and was irritated when Emily laughed under her breath, embarrassed.

'Nothing.'

'Out with it.'

'Well, he says that you'll end up covered in cobwebs if you're not careful, married to a dreary bank manager who likes his meals at the same time every day and gets in a flap if his routine's thrown out of joint.'

'Tell your father thanks very much for plotting my life,' Rebecca said coldly. 'I'm surprised he has the time, considering how active he is on the social front.'

'Oh, all that's finished. I haven't seen a bimbo for at least a week.'

'He's probably resting.' She had had enough of hearing about Nicholas, but was masochistically tempted to prolong the agony by asking a few more pointless questions. 'Between jobs.' She gave a cynical laugh.

'What are you up to anyway?' Emily asked easily, and Rebecca would have sworn that there was amusement in her voice.

'Actually, *actually*, it's all happening up here for me,' Rebecca said viciously. 'Next week, I shall be starting a new job until I get my old one back and I shall be viewing a couple of houses. I intend to be a home owner. One of the houses looks marvellous. A bit expensive for me, but just the thing. It's a cottage, out in the countryside, and it seems perfect.'

She described where it was for Emily in glowing detail. Hearing herself, she wondered whether she was talking about the same place which, according to the specification, was in need of some minor repair work, particular attention to the roof, looked as though its last brush with paint had been decades previously and had a front garden that loosely resembled your average forest. 'Hence the cheap price!' the estate agent had informed her cheerfully. 'It's a bargain.'

'Oh, that sounds great,' Emily said, disappointed.

'It's fabulous!' If her voice got any shriller, it would be off the scale. 'Anyway, my love, if I *do* get this place—' *Which I won't because even though it does look charming it's still too expensive, bargain or no bargain* '—you'll be the first guest. You'll have to bring a paintbrush.' *Not to mention your DIY roof-repair kit and a heavy-duty lawn-mower.* 'Must dash now, anyway. I've got plans for this evening,' she added mysteriously.

'What *kind* of plans?'

Oh, the usual. Girlfriend over for a meal. Then a spot of telly, followed by a few pages of my novel and then hours in bed thinking of your wretched father. 'Of the tall, handsome, non-bank manager variety!' she said gaily.

So Emily sounded crestfallen by the end of the conversation, but if she *did* report back to Nicholas, then at least he would hear a version of her life that sounded wildly exciting and fulfilled. She regretted that she hadn't gone into a bit more fabricated detail about the handsome stranger who wasn't a bank manager, but lies, even of the white variety, were so foreign to her that she hadn't been thinking on her feet.

Bank manager indeed. Dreary indeed. Cobwebs indeed. How dared he? How dared he sit in his glamorous house, surrounded by a bevy of glamorous women and pass judgement on her lifestyle? And, worse, confide in Emily!

The job, which turned out to be more demanding than her previous one at the boarding-school, lived up to its promise of distraction. It distracted her from the housework, from making phone calls to her friends, from her two-hour evening routine in front of the television and from remembering to do certain essential things, such as buy food. Unfortunately, it was not enough of a distraction to stop her thinking about Nicholas.

She found herself wondering what Nicholas would say if she were to describe some of her students and fellow teachers. She found herself thinking a little too hard and a little too often about the way he would smile, or say something witty and then pull her towards him and bury his face in her hair.

Without seeing the house, she made up her mind to buy it. She had a fair amount of savings and if the mortgage was a little hefty to start with she would soon grow accustomed to tightening her belt. She wove dreamy fantasies of doing up the property, room by room, filling each one with all her favourite colours. She had loved her mother's little council house, with its cosy greens and terracottas. On the evening before she was due to view the place, she sat down with the little scaled diagram of its innards and worked out what she would do. The estate agent had been right. It was a bargain. It was in a perfect location and all it needed would be a little love and lots of time.

In all events, Rebecca felt that she had both to spare.

She had managed to persuade herself so successfully into this pleasant imaginary scenario that when the telephone rang at half past nine, and she picked it up to hear the estate agent's voice on the line, she was half tempted to make an offer in anticipation of getting it. She was shocked when, after a few pleasantries, he said sheepishly, 'I'm afraid I may have some bad news for you. We have a cash buyer for the house who's prepared to pay the full asking price.'

'No, that's impossible,' Rebecca said calmly. The house was going to be her therapy. Now that she could see it vanishing into the mist, she was even more determined to hang on to it.

'I'm afraid not. It's quite remarkable, considering it's been on the market for four months. Lots of viewers, but none prepared to take on the commitment of doing the necessary work to get it up and running, and now two people seriously interested, one interested enough to buy unseen.' He paused. 'I *did* mention to the gentleman that you were due to view the place tomorrow morning at nine, and he indicated that you should go ahead. If you fell in love with it and were prepared to meet his offer, then he would allow you to have it.'

'Let me get this right. The man offers full price for a dilapidated cottage in the middle of nowhere, then says that I can have it if I like it provided I can match his price. Has it occurred to you that that kind of behaviour is a little unorthodox? Have you stopped to consider that you might be doing business with a lunatic? Why would he pay full price for a house and then be prepared to let me have it if I like it?'

'Apparently, this is to be a second house for him, so it's not life or death if he doesn't get it. I explained to him that you had seen the particulars and were very keen, and that you were living in rented accommodation, so he recognises that your need is greater than his, I suppose.'

'Very magnanimous of him, I'm sure,' Rebecca said sarcastically. The cottage, which she had begun to think of as hers, was disappearing, and with it was going her future and her therapeutic recovery from Nicholas Knight.

'If you'd like to cancel the viewing...I'm sure something else will come up very soon. In fact, I have three new places which have just come in, all within your price range.' There was a shuffling-of-papers sound over the line. 'More modern properties, so that could well be an advantage because you could walk straight in with no work to be done.'

I need the challenge of doing a place up, Rebecca thought despairingly. I don't need modern. 'I'll view it as arranged.'

'Fine. In that case, I'll meet you there in the morning. Nine o'clock.'

But as she drove there the following morning the glitter of the place had been tarnished. She wouldn't get it. She couldn't afford the full price and she was pretty sure that her rival buyer was aware of that. Even offering a few thousand less than the asking price would have stretched her financial resources to the absolute limit.

It was a bitter pill to swallow, and made even more bitter by her first glimpse of the cottage, which nestled among a tangle of weeds and overgrown bush and looked even more delightful in reality than it had in the glossy-printed cover picture. In fact, it looked like something out of a fairy tale, small, sepia-coloured and really, for its price, ridiculously expensive, which was probably why it had not been snapped up. It would have been too tiny for a family, but too expensive for a single person, unless, Rebecca conceded wryly, that single person was an emotional mess with a healthy savings account.

There was a battered Land Rover parked in the drive, which meant that Gerry, her unreliable estate agent, was already inside, and without knocking she pushed open the front door into a small hallway with cupboard-sized rooms on either side. Cobwebs hung from the exposed beams and, peering around her, she noticed several broken panes of glass in the windows.

'Hello!' she called out in a ringing voice. 'Mr Hackman? Are you here?'

'Upstairs!' came a muffled voice, and she tentatively made her way up the stairs, pausing to look down behind her and already envisaging what she would have done had the cottage been hers.

'In here!'

She made her way to the sound of the voice, pushed open a bedroom door and was confronted with the extraordinary sight of a room in which a sumptuous four-poster bed stood with its back to an oak-panelled wall. Disconcertingly, there was a squat table by the window, on which there was a bottle of champagne and two glasses.

She took in this bizarre scene and felt uneasy prickles climb up the back of her spine.

'Mr Hackman?' she asked timidly.

'Not quite.' She saw the shadow before she saw the man, coming out at her from behind the door, and she gasped in horror, suddenly filled with panic. She felt the room begin to spin, closed her eyes and seconds later came round to the sound of a man saying in an amused drawl, 'I would never have thought that you were the fainting kind.'

Her eyelids flickered and she opened her eyes and struggled to sit up, but he was pinning her down by her wrists.

'What are *you* doing here?' she asked with shocked disbelief. 'God, this must be a dream.'

She closed her eyes again, and he leaned over her and said softly, 'No dream. I'm real. Pinch me if you like.'

Rebecca didn't. Instead she took a deep breath and opened her eyes, steadily looking at him, trying to read his intentions.

'You're the buyer, aren't you?' she said dully. 'Emily told you about my plans to buy this cottage and you immediately got on the phone to the estate agent and did the one thing you knew would hurt me. You bought it. How could you?' She was blinking back her tears and her voice had become shaky.

'Shh,' he murmured, smiling.

'I am not going to shut up,' she began, working herself into a lather and renewing her attempts to struggle into a sitting position. In a feat of strength, he had managed to manoeuvre her when she had fainted on to the bed, and she sincerely hoped that he had pulled a few ligaments for his trouble.

'Oh, yes, you are,' he told her firmly, 'You're going to

stop putting two and two together and getting five and you're going to shut up and let me talk.'

'Or else?'

'Or else I shall give in to my baser instincts and ravish you.'

That reduced her to silence and she stared at him, dumbfounded.

'You asked me what I'm doing here. Well, I'll tell you.' He inhaled deeply and then exhaled on a sigh. 'Since France, I've been to hell and back. When I first saw you again, at the school, I was amused to see how little you'd changed, and amused to find that against all odds I fancied you as much as I did when we were younger.

'When you hit me with the bombshell that Emily was pregnant and then launched into your oblique attack on me as being an indirect cause of my daughter's behaviour patterns, I could have throttled you, but for the first time, with a woman, your mind attracted me as much as your body. When I offered you the job to tutor Emily, I'm ashamed to admit that a part of me was curious to get to know you again. Just seeing you had been enough to bring back a flood of memories and it was surprising how detailed they all were.'

She could sympathise with that. Her whole body was rigid with tension and he still hadn't got around to telling her why he had bought the cottage.

'Can I sit up, please? I'm getting pins and needles in my arms.' It was prosaic, but it did the job. He released her and she sat bolt upright, feeling ridiculous to be on a bed still wearing her formal shoes and thick suit which she had donned in the hope that Gerry Hackman, who was only her age or even younger, would see her as a serious contender for the prize and not a dim-witted girl on her own who could be easily outmanoeuvred.

She rubbed her wrists.

'Shall I kiss them better?' he asked. 'I have magic lips.'

She knew all about his magic lips and she tilted her head aggressively to look at him. The aggression turned to uncertainty when she saw the expression in his eyes: a certain warmth and tenderness that made her tremble.

'It won't work,' she forced herself to say, and he frowned at her with incomprehension.

'What won't work?'

'This!' Rebecca waved her arm vaguely to encompass the room. 'You can't blackmail me into sleeping with you, Nicholas. You can't buy this house and then offer it back to me on your terms, if that's what all this is about.' She tensely waited for his flare of anger, but instead he shook his head in wonderment.

'Between you and Emily I don't know which of you baffles me more. I don't intend to *blackmail* you into sleeping with me.' He laughed dryly. 'And that's an insult to my ego, in case you hadn't noticed. I bought this cottage because I've finally come to my senses.'

'You mean you've finally decided that owning a place in the country is what you need?'

'Don't be flippant,' he said without any rancour. 'This is hard enough for me as it is.'

But what else could she be? Rebecca wondered. She knew that her flippancy was self-defence, and she knew that she had to defend herself or else lay herself open to yet more hurt and pain. Whatever point Nicholas was working up to, she would bet that it would not be what she wanted to hear.

'When we were in France...'

'I know, I don't want to talk about it. It happened. These things sometimes do. We're two consenting adults.'

'Do you mind?'

'What?'

'Not jumping in with both feet? I came here with my rehearsed declaration and neither of us is budging until I've said it from start to finish.' He brushed a strand of hair from her face and she pulled away sharply. If he noticed her reaction, he gave no indication of it.

'But I know why you're doing that,' he murmured, and although she clicked her tongue and raised her eyes skywards her indifference was undermined by the furious colour charging up her face. She could feel her heart battering against her ribcage and her throat was dry. It was just as well that he had consigned the speaking part to himself because she seriously doubted she could have harnessed her vocal cords into doing anything.

'You're scared, aren't you? Scared of being hurt? Scared of your own vulnerability? Everyone's vulnerable and there's nothing to be afraid of.'

Something emerged from her throat. It sounded like a croak.

'You're scared because you've fallen in love with me. Aren't you?'

Rebecca squeezed her eyes tightly shut.

'And don't go fainting on me again,' he warned. She didn't have to look at his face to know that it wore an expression of smug satisfaction. He had ferreted out her secret, either by inspired guesswork or just instinct, and now that he had he would move in for the kill. Was that why he had come here?

'Open your eyes,' he ordered, and she reluctantly opened them and looked at him resentfully. 'You're pouting,' he said with amused surprise.

'I am not pouting. I just want to go now.'

'When we're finally getting somewhere?'

'We're not getting anywhere!' she protested desperately.

'Oh, yes, we are.' He couldn't stop himself. He couldn't conceal the expression of sheer pleasure on his face and Rebecca felt tears of mortification spring to her eyes.

'My darling Rebecca,' he said huskily, raising one hand to her face and tracing the outline of her mouth with his finger. By now, she was breathing so fast that she sounded, to her own dismayed ears, like a woman in labour.

'Don't,' she pleaded. 'You've come here to gloat and you've had your moment of triumph.'

'I've come here to tell you that I love you,' he whispered. 'And I'm not gloating. I'm merely smiling because suddenly the world is a wonderful place.'

World. Wonderful. Love. Not gloating. All the words jumbled together in her head, until they were spinning around so quickly that she could pin none of them down.

'What did you say?' she whispered. She decided that if this was a dream after all, then she wanted to stay put, at least for ever.

'I never expected to fall in love,' he said quietly. 'In fact, in all my relationships with women, whatever the duration, love had never been something that had crept around the door. Fun, sex and then amicable farewells. Then along you came with your forthright, no-nonsense air and your preconceived notions and without even realising it I found myself getting addicted to your company, addicted to the way you laughed, as though you almost didn't want to but just couldn't help yourself, addicted to the way you looked and the feel of you.' He sighed and made a wry face.

'France,' he said, 'which was the restorative cure for Emily, turned out to be mine too. For the first time in my life, I felt completely relaxed. I even forgot about work!' He laughed as though amazed that such an eventuality could occur. 'And it wasn't just France and all that rustic beauty. I was you. You made me feel like a boy again.'

'Why didn't you tell me this weeks ago?' she asked, bemused and still too frightened of disappointment to join him in this wonderful glow he had created.

'Because I've never been in love before, because I didn't *want* to be in love.' He paused and looked her directly in the eye. 'You're not the only one who's cautious, you know. I went through one marriage to a woman I ended up despising. I wasn't willing to face the fact that...'

'That what?' She leaned forward, needing his reply as much as she had ever needed anything in her life before.

'That I wanted to try the wretched institution again.'

'You don't mean that.'

'Will you marry me?'

Rebecca thought that she might faint again, or at least swoon, if swoon wasn't a ridiculous word when applied to a strapping woman like herself.

'And what about all those bimbos?'

'They were a complete waste of time. I did it to get you jealous and I suppose to prove that women wanted me, even if you didn't.'

She felt an overwhelming love for him and impulsively reached up to stroke his face. He captured her hand in his and turned it over, kissing the underside of her wrist, then pulling her fingers, one by one, into his mouth.

She felt weeks of denied yearning spread through her veins like molten lava.

'So, answer my question. Will you marry me?'

'I shall seriously consider it,' she laughed, and he pushed her down on the bed.

'I can be very persuasive,' he murmured, nibbling her ear and stroking the length of her thighs, which meant doing battle with her tights and skirt.

'Hence the bed?'

'I wanted to overpower you. It was a cheap stunt but it was the best that we could come up with.'

'We…?'

'I think it's fair to say that Emily will be thrilled.' He grinned. 'Whoever said that women don't always end up getting their own way?'

Yes, Rebecca thought, sailing away to paradise as her body became hot under his searching caresses, I did.

MILLS & BOON®

Makes any time special

Enjoy a romantic novel from Mills & Boon®

Presents...™   *Enchanted™*   TEMPTATION.

Historical Romance™   ♥ **MEDICAL ROMANCE®**

COMING NEXT MONTH

MILLS & BOON®
Presents...™

THE BRIDEGROOM'S DILEMMA by *Lindsay Armstrong*

When Skye admitted she longed to have children, just weeks before their wedding, Nick couldn't hide his doubts. When Skye walked away he was devastated. Now Nick must convince Skye to give their love another chance…

HUSBAND ON TRUST by *Jacqueline Baird*

In the seven weeks since their whirlwind wedding, gorgeous entrepreneur Alex Solomos has transformed Lisa's life. She tells herself she's being foolish for thinking it's all too good to last—until she makes two shocking discoveries…

THE ONE-WEEK BABY by *Hayley Gardner*

When a baby boy was left on West Gallagher's doorstep, Annie was there to help out, and in doing so she fell in love. West, however, had vowed never to have a family. But perhaps looking after little Teddy might help change his mind…

THE TAMING OF TYLER KINCAID by *Sandra Marton*

Who is Tyler Kincaid? And why does he think he can lay claim to Jonas Baron's Texan ranch, Espada—and Jonas's stepdaughter, Caitlin? She wants Tyler—but will he ever reveal the secret quest that has bought him to Espada?

Available from 3rd March 2000

COMING NEXT MONTH

MILLS & BOON®

Presents...™

MARRIAGE BY CONTRACT *by Margaret Mayo*

When Nicole answered a 'wife wanted' advertisement, she found herself agreeing to marry mysterious Ross Dufrais. Secrets aside, what neither of them could conceal was the fierce attraction they shared...

A BRIDE TO BE *by Kristin Morgan*

According to the terms of her grandfather's will, Brie and Drew have to get married. However, as Brie's intense dislike of Drew is surpassed only by an intense attraction, she's determined theirs will only be a temporary arrangement...

THEIR ENGAGEMENT IS ANNOUNCED
by Carole Mortimer

To avoid his mother's matchmaking Griffin Sinclair had announced that he was going to marry Dora Baxter. She had to play along with the pretence—but it wasn't going to be easy as Dora had secretly been in love with Griffin for years...

THE WEDDING DATE *by Christie Ridgway*

Emma had no intention of attending her ex-fiancé's wedding alone, so she invited handsome stranger, Trick Webster. By the time they got to the kiss, suddenly one date was nowhere near enough...

Available from 3rd March 2000

FREE!

4 Books
and a surprise gift!

We would like to take this opportunity to thank you for reading this Mills & Boon® book by offering you the chance to take FOUR more specially selected titles from the Presents...™ series absolutely FREE! We're also making this offer to introduce you to the benefits of the Reader Service™—

★ FREE home delivery
★ FREE gifts and competitions
★ FREE monthly Newsletter
★ Books available before they're in the shops
★ Exclusive Reader Service discounts

Accepting these FREE books and gift places you under no obligation to buy; you may cancel at any time, even after receiving your free shipment. Simply complete your details below and return the entire page to the address below. *You don't even need a stamp!*

YES! Please send me 4 free Presents...™ books and a surprise gift. I understand that unless you hear from me, I will receive 6 superb new titles every month for just £2.40 each, postage and packing free. I am under no obligation to purchase any books and may cancel my subscription at any time. The free books and gift will be mine to keep in any case.

POEB

Ms/Mrs/Miss/Mr ....Initials ....
BLOCK CAPITALS PLEASE

Surname ....

Address ....

....

....Postcode ....

Send this whole page to:
UK: The Reader Service, FREEPOST CN81, Croydon, CR9 3WZ
EIRE: The Reader Service, PO Box 4546, Kilcock, County Kildare (stamp required)

Offer not valid to current Reader Service subscribers to this series. We reserve the right to refuse an application and applicants must be aged 18 years or over. Only one application per household. Terms and prices subject to change without notice. Offer expires 31st August 2000. As a result of this application, you may receive further offers from Harlequin Mills & Boon Limited and other carefully selected companies. If you would prefer not to share in this opportunity please write to The Data Manager at the address above.

Mills & Boon is a registered trademark owned by Harlequin Mills & Boon Limited.
Presents... is being used as a trademark.